YOU CANNOT ESCAPE WHAT YOU'VE BECOME

PARASITE'S EMBRACE

NEELANSH

BLUEROSE PUBLISHERS
U.K.

Copyright © Neelansh 2025

All rights reserved by author. No part of this publication may be reproduced, stored in a retrieval system or transmitted in any form or by any means, electronic, mechanical, photocopying, recording or otherwise, without the prior permission of the author. Although every precaution has been taken to verify the accuracy of the information contained herein, the publisher assumes no responsibility for any errors or omissions. No liability is assumed for damages that may result from the use of information contained within.

BlueRose Publishers takes no responsibility for any damages, losses, or liabilities that may arise from the use or misuse of the information, products, or services provided in this publication.

For permissions requests or inquiries regarding this publication, please contact:

BLUEROSE PUBLISHERS
www.BlueRoseONE.com
info@bluerosepublishers.com
+4407342408967

ISBN: 978-93-7139-670-7

Cover design: Daksh
Typesetting: Tanya Raj Upadhyay

First Edition: June 2025

Author's Note

Stories have a way of revealing truths we often overlook, and *Parasites' Embrace* is no exception. At its core, this is a story about control—about how easily the mind can be shaped, molded, and led to believe in a reality that may not be its own. It explores the unsettling idea that the greatest form of control isn't force, but **conviction**—when someone is so deeply manipulated that they believe their choices are their own.

Liam and Nari are not your typical protagonists. They aren't rebels fighting against a system, nor are they aware of the full extent of their situation. They are agents of a force that has convinced them they are on the right side of history. Their choices feel like their own, their missions feel justified, and the truth is buried beneath layers of illusions. What makes their journey compelling is not whether they can break free—but whether they even realize they need to.

One of the most fascinating elements of this story, to me, is the role of the parasites. They are not just mindless invaders; they are strategists, operating under a belief system that justifies their methods. They are not evil in the traditional sense—they are simply efficient. They do what needs to be done, eliminating doubt, fear, and conflict by ensuring their hosts never question their purpose. And yet, within all of this, something remains untouched: love. The one thing the parasites cannot fully rewrite.

Love, in its purest form, is irrational. It does not fit into logic or grand calculations, and that is what makes it powerful. No matter how much the parasites manipulate Liam and Nari, no matter how much of their thoughts and beliefs are rewritten, their love remains a whisper of their true selves—a small, unbreakable fragment of who they used to be. It does not save them. It does not lead them to rebellion. But it exists, stubbornly, as a quiet defiance against absolute control.

I have always been drawn to stories where the lines between right and wrong are blurred, where characters are not simply heroes or villains, but people shaped by their circumstances. This book is not about victory. It is about understanding—about what it means to lose yourself and whether, in the end, ignorance truly is bliss. Because sometimes, the happiest ending isn't escape—it's accepting the illusion as reality.

Table of Contents

Chapter 1: The Bond That Couldn't Be Broken ... 1

   Years earlier. The Spy Training Facility. 2

   Paris – The Bloodstained Alley 3

   Berlin – The Fire and the Smoke 5

   Seoul – Present Day 6

Chapter 2: Parasitic Threat 9

   Mission Briefing: The Target 16

Chapter 3: The Transformation 18

   The Transformation 20

   Morning Routine and Meeting at Headquarters ... 22

   At Headquarters 24

Chapter 4: The Unseen Shift 25

   A Disquieting Change 26

   An Unexpected Encounter 27

   Liam Investigates 28

Chapter 5: The Dreamland of Truth 30

   The Dreamland 32

   The Depths of the Mind 34

Awakening.. 36

Chapter 6: The Factory's Secret 38

Into the Shadows 38

The Horrifying Discovery 40

Chapter 7: Seven Days of Shadows 46

Day 1: The First Step into Darkness..................... 46

Day 2: The Whisper Network 49

Day 3: Ghosts in the Machine 51

Day 4: The Assassin's Trail 53

Day 5: The Firewall of Deception 60

Day 6: A Night at the Club 65

Day 7: The Turn of Mind....................................... 71

Chapter 8: Captured in the Shadows................... 76

Chapter 9: The Final Stand 83

Chapter 10: The Revelation 92

The Lost History of Nikri....................................... 98

Chapter 11: The Choice.. 103

Chapter 12: The Rebirth 109

Chapter 13: Reunion and New Purpose 115

Chapter 14: Fractured Allegiances 119

Part 1: Shadows in the Glass 119

Part 2: The Illusion of Free Will 120

Part 3: Fractures in the System 122

Part 4: The Parasite's Mercy..............................123

Part 5: The Weight of Acceptance 125

Chapter 15: The Prophecy Revealed-
A Cosmic Deception **126**

Epilogue: Love's Eternal Symphony **131**

Chapter 1:
The Bond That Couldn't Be Broken

The city lights of Seoul shimmered against the rain-slicked streets, casting neon reflections that stretched endlessly into the night. The world moved fast, yet in the dimly lit rooftop café, time seemed to slow. It was one of those rare moments where Liam and Nari could simply exist—no missions, no directives, just them. Across the table, their eyes remained locked, an unspoken understanding passing between them. The hum of distant traffic, the faint chatter of late-night wanderers—it all faded into the background.

Liam leaned back slightly, his sharp brown eyes scanning Nari's face with a knowing smirk. He was tall, broad-shouldered, with a strong jawline and jet-black hair that was always slightly tousled, no matter how many times he ran a hand through it. There was something about him that commanded attention—his quiet confidence, his intense gaze, the way he moved with the effortless precision of someone who had spent years honing his body into a weapon.

Nari, on the other hand, was a study in contrast. Her presence was quiet yet powerful, wrapped in an air of graceful mystery. Her long, sleek black hair framed delicate but sharp features—a small nose, full lips, and dark brown eyes that turned molten gold in the right light. She was smaller than Liam, but every movement she made was deliberate, precise. There was no wasted energy, no unnecessary flourish. Every step, every glance, every breath was calculated—a skill honed through years of training and survival.

The air between them was thick with something unspoken. A delicate tension, fragile yet unyielding, humming like an electric wire stretched to its limit. Liam's fingers toyed idly with the rim of his coffee cup, the steam curling into the cold night air like the whispers of a ghost. Nari's gaze flickered downward for the briefest of moments before meeting his again with unwavering intensity.

Years earlier. The Spy Training Facility.

A harsh fluorescent glow bathed the underground training hall. The scent of sweat, leather, and blood tinged the air. Liam and Nari, both young recruits, stood in the combat ring, bruised and sweating from relentless sparring.

INSTRUCTOR: Again!

Liam lunged, Nari countered—a perfect match. Every strike was met with equal force, neither willing to back down. But Liam's smirk gave him away—he was enjoying this.

NARI: You're holding back.

LIAM: Maybe I just like watching you win.

The first time they had met, it had been less than friendly. A high-stakes mission had forced them into an uneasy alliance, their initial distrust of one another threatening to get them both killed. But when the bullets started flying, Liam had seen something in Nari that he had never seen in anyone before—an unwavering resolve, a quiet fire that burned beneath her composed exterior. And she had seen something in him too—a man who was willing to take a bullet if it meant protecting someone he cared about.

Their bond was tested time and time again. Missions turned deadly, betrayals loomed, and yet they always came back to each other.

Paris – The Bloodstained Alley

The rain had been relentless that night. The cobblestone streets of Montmartre glistened under the streetlamps, their glow distorted by water streaming down the pavement. They were meant to extract a high-value target from a secret meeting in an underground wine cellar. Simple. Clean. Until it wasn't.

Gunfire erupted as soon as they reached the extraction point. The target had been compromised. The mission was a setup.

Nari had barely dodged a bullet when Liam grabbed her wrist and pulled her into a narrow alleyway. His back pressed against the damp brick wall, his breath uneven but steady. Nari was bleeding—a deep gash along her ribs. She hissed, trying to move, but Liam's grip tightened.

"Hold still." His voice was edged with something she rarely heard—panic.

Nari gritted her teeth. "It's just a scratch."

Liam's jaw clenched as he pressed a gloved hand over the wound. Blood seeped through his fingers, warm and sticky against the cold air. His eyes locked onto hers, frustration warring with something deeper. "We aren't supposed to get attached," she whispered, her voice weaker than she wanted it to be.

Liam only gritted his teeth. "Too late."

They had made it out, barely. But the sight of Nari bleeding in his arms had burned itself into his mind. From that moment on, Liam knew—she wasn't just his partner. She was his reason.

Berlin – The Fire and the Smoke

One year later, they were in Berlin. The cold air carried the scent of smoke and distant sirens. What was meant to be a routine extraction of stolen intel turned into a massacre when an ambush forced them into a collapsing building.

Liam had shouted Nari's name when the explosion tore through the structure. A second too late. She had been buried beneath twisted steel and concrete.

For twenty agonizing seconds, Liam had believed she was gone. The fire illuminated the destruction around him as he clawed through the debris with shaking hands. And then—he found her. Bruised. Coughing. Alive.

He pulled her free, cradling her against his chest, his grip unrelenting. "You idiot," he breathed, relief and anger mixing in his tone. "You were supposed to stay behind."

Nari, still gasping for air, managed a smirk. "Since when do I listen?"

For the first time in his life, Liam felt something terrifying. Vulnerability. If she had died that night, a part of him would have too. He held her tighter, as if anchoring himself to the reality that she was still there.

Seoul – Present Day

The weight of those moments still lingered between them, unspoken but understood. Sitting across from each other in the rooftop café, the world outside faded away.

Liam finally spoke, his voice a whisper against the night air. "That night in Berlin… I thought I lost you."

Nari studied him, her expression unreadable. Then, softly, "And if I had?"

His fingers curled around the handle of his cup. "Then I wouldn't be here."

A pause. The weight of his words settled between them. Nari reached out, her fingertips brushing against his hand. The briefest of touches, but it was enough.

Their love had never been spoken aloud, never acknowledged outright. It was there in the way Liam covered for her when she was exhausted after back-to-back missions. It was in the way Nari always positioned herself between Liam and an approaching threat, ready to take a hit before letting him get hurt. It was in the stolen glances, the hands brushing together too long, the quiet acceptance that they belonged to each other in a world where attachments were dangerous.

One night, after a particularly grueling mission, they had found themselves in a safe house overlooking the Tokyo skyline. The city lights shimmered against the glass, their reflections interwoven like two halves of the same whole. Liam had poured them each a drink, the silence between them comfortable but heavy with unspoken words.

"No matter what happens," he had said, his voice steady, "I'll always choose you."

Nari had met his gaze, unwavering. "And I'll always bring you back, no matter how lost you get."

And that was how it always was with them. In a world full of deception, their love was the one thing they never had to question.

They didn't need promises. They didn't need words. They only needed each other.

Their lives had always been tangled in secrecy, but their love was the only truth that mattered.

The night stretched on, and the world outside continued its ceaseless hum, oblivious to the storm that brewed within them. But for now, they were just Liam and Nari—two souls bound together by fate, tethered by a love that even the darkness could not erode.

In their world of deception, lies, and shifting allegiances, this—whatever it was between them—was the only thing that felt real.

Their time together was always temporary, fleeting moments stolen between missions, but they made each second count. Because deep down, they both knew the truth—one day, the mission would come first. And when that day arrived, neither of them would have a choice.

Chapter 2: Parasitic Threat

The sun blazed mercilessly over the dusty streets of Mexico City, casting long shadows across the crumbling rooftops. The air smelled of gasoline, sweat, and impending violence. Somewhere below, in a heavily fortified compound, Ricardo Mendez, one of the most ruthless drug lords in the world, sat inside his office, unaware that his empire was about to fall.

Liam crouched on a rooftop, his pulse steady, his breathing controlled. Through the scope of his rifle, he watched Mendez laugh, a thick cigar dangling from his lips, surrounded by his heavily armed men. Each of them had a reputation for brutality, but Liam wasn't concerned with their pasts—only their impending deaths.

He waited for the signal.

A sharp click in his earpiece. Go.

Liam moved with practiced ease, dropping down silently into the alley below. The first guard never saw him coming—Liam's knife slid effortlessly between his ribs before he could scream. He caught the body, lowering it gently to the ground before slipping through the compound's outer defenses. Two more guards patrolled the perimeter. He took them down with swift precision—one silenced shot, one brutal strike to the throat.

He was inside.

The compound was a maze of corridors, dimly lit by flickering bulbs. The sounds of drunken laughter echoed from a nearby room—Mendez's men, indulging in their final moments of ignorance. Liam moved past them, his footsteps soundless against the concrete floor. His target was in the main office, guarded by Hector Salazar, a behemoth of a man, Mendez's most trusted enforcer.

Liam found him waiting just outside the office door, arms crossed over his massive chest.

"You shouldn't be here, amigo," Salazar growled, cracking his knuckles.

Liam exhaled. "And yet, here I am."

Salazar lunged, throwing a punch that could shatter bone. Liam ducked, countering with a lightning-fast kick to the ribs. The impact barely fazed the brute. They exchanged blows, brutal and efficient. Salazar fought like a bear—powerful, unrelenting. Liam fought like a ghost—quick, precise, untouchable.

A final strike—a blade to the thigh, a knee to the jaw—Salazar crumpled. Liam kicked open the office door.

Mendez looked up, startled, his cigar falling from his lips. "Wait, we can—"

A single shot silenced him forever.

Within minutes, the compound was ablaze, an inferno consuming the empire Mendez had built with blood and betrayal. As Liam disappeared into the night, sirens wailed in the distance.

Mission complete.

The hum of fluorescent lights buzzed softly overhead, casting an eerie glow over the sleek, modern interior of the intelligence headquarters. The air was thick with an unspoken tension, the kind that preceded war. Monitors flickered along the walls, displaying an endless stream of encrypted messages, satellite imagery, and classified dossiers. It was the kind of place where silence spoke louder than words, where every individual carried secrets too heavy to bear. On the glass panel near the entrance, someone had scratched three interlocking rings—small, almost unnoticeable. Liam's eyes lingered on them for a moment. Something about the symbol felt familiar, like a half-remembered dream, but before he could dwell on it, his gaze shifted back to the intelligence reports in his hands.

Liam sat in the briefing room, absently spinning a sleek pen between his fingers. His brown eyes, sharp as ever, flickered over the latest intelligence reports. Another assassination order. Another target. Another mission where he was expected to act without hesitation, without question. His entire life had been spent following orders. That was the job. That was the code. And yet, something gnawed at the back of his mind—a whisper of doubt he couldn't shake.

He wasn't alone for long.

The doors to the main office burst open, slamming against the walls with a resounding crash. In strode a hulking figure, a man whose mere presence seemed to suck the oxygen from the room. Viktor Kross. Seven feet tall, built like a freight train, with scars that told stories no one dared to ask about. His heavy combat boots thudded against the marble floor, and his deep, guttural voice cut through the hushed atmosphere like a blade.

"Where the hell is she?" Kross growled, his Russian accent thick, his bloodshot eyes scanning the room wildly.

Agents instinctively reached for their weapons, fingers hovering over holsters. Liam, however, remained seated, his expression unreadable. He knew exactly who Kross was looking for—Nari.

"You don't get to storm in here and make demands," Liam said calmly, setting his pen down. "This isn't your battleground."

Kross' nostrils flared, his muscular arms flexing as if preparing for a fight. "Don't play games with me, kid. I know she's here. And I know she's been tracking my operations. If she doesn't back off, there will be consequences."

Liam rose slowly, meeting the giant man's glare without flinching. "That sounds an awful lot like a threat."

Kross chuckled darkly. "You're damn right it is."

Before anyone could react, Kross swung. His massive fist rocketed toward Liam's head with the force of a wrecking ball. But Liam was fast—faster than Kross anticipated. He ducked just in time, pivoting on his heel and driving a solid kick into the brute's ribs.

Kross barely staggered, but the impact was enough to make him pause.

The room erupted into chaos. Agents shouted, weapons were drawn, but before anyone could fire a shot, the doors to the office swung open once more. Lady Boss.

Tall, imposing, with a presence that could freeze a man mid-step, Eleanor Graves, known only as Lady Boss, entered the room, her piercing gaze locking onto Kross like a predator sizing up prey. Behind her, the CEO himself, Stanley Vale, followed, his expression cold, calculated.

"That's enough," Lady Boss commanded, her voice sharp as ice. "Viktor, if you have a problem, you bring it to me, not my agents."

Kross exhaled sharply through his nose, glaring at Liam before stepping back. "Then tell your agent to stay out of my way."

Lady Boss offered a tight-lipped smile. "We'll discuss it later. Now get out."

Kross lingered for a moment before finally turning and striding out of the room. The moment he was gone, Lady Boss turned to Liam, her eyes narrowing slightly. "You handled that well."

Liam exhaled, rolling his shoulders. "Wasn't exactly difficult."

The CEO stepped forward, clearing his throat. "We didn't call you in today to handle Kross. We have a mission for you. A critical one."

Liam straightened, his posture instinctively rigid. "I'm listening."

Lady Boss placed a file on the table, sliding it toward him. "There's a new threat. One unlike anything we've dealt with before. We're assigning you to eliminate it."

Liam flipped the folder open, his brow furrowing as he scanned the contents. At first, the reports looked standard—targets, locations, movements. But then he reached the classified photos. His stomach twisted.

The victims. Their eyes were glowing, unnaturally bright. Their skin pale, their expressions eerily serene even in death. Something was wrong.

"What am I looking at?" Liam asked, his voice quieter than he intended.

Lady Boss exchanged a glance with the CEO. "We're dealing with a parasitic entity. Something that takes control of its host's mind. Makes them stronger, faster, deadlier."

Liam's blood ran cold. "And you want me to—"

"Kill them," Lady Boss confirmed. "Before this infection spreads."

Liam sat in silence, staring at the images. There was something deeply unsettling about them, something that made his instincts scream at him that this mission was different. More dangerous. More…wrong.

But he had his orders.

And Liam had never disobeyed an order before.

He closed the folder, exhaling sharply. "When do I start?"

The CEO smiled. "Immediately."

Mission Briefing: The Target

Liam took a deep breath as he scanned the final pages of the report. The parasite was spreading fast. Multiple confirmed hosts had already disappeared into the city, and the risk of an outbreak was growing by the hour. His mission was to track and eliminate them before they could take over more civilians.

The briefing contained the names of suspected hosts. Former intelligence officers, high-ranking politicians, even elite mercenaries—somehow, the parasite was choosing its victims strategically. This wasn't just an infection. This was a takeover. And buried within the classified reports, there was a single ominous line, one that intelligence had dismissed as irrelevant— "When the loyal fall and the rings align, the true cycle will begin."

"Your first target," Lady Boss continued, "is someone you've worked with before. Agent Damian Grinn ."

Liam stiffened. Damian had been one of the best. Smart. Fast. Loyal. If he had fallen to this thing, that meant no one was safe.

Lady Boss watched him carefully. "Can you do this?"

Liam shut the file, his jaw tightening. "Yes."

The mission had begun.

Chapter 3:
The Transformation

The sky above the city was a vast canvas of midnight blue, sprinkled with distant stars that flickered like whispered secrets. The streets below pulsed with life—neon signs flashing, the hum of traffic, and the distant melody of a street performer's violin. From the rooftop of a high-rise safe house, Liam and Nari sat side by side, their legs dangling over the edge. It was a rare moment of peace, stolen from a world that never truly rested.

Nari tilted her head back, her sleek black hair cascading behind her as she inhaled the crisp night air. "Do you ever think about what life would've been like if we weren't… this?" she asked, her voice a soft murmur.

Liam glanced at her, his sharp brown eyes reflecting the city lights. "What, if we weren't spies? If we didn't spend our nights chasing shadows?"

She nodded, her fingers absentmindedly tracing the edge of the ledge beneath her. "Yeah. Just… normal. Maybe we'd be regular people with boring jobs, complaining about deadlines and traffic instead of tracking terrorists and dodging bullets." She let out a soft chuckle, but then her voice dropped into something quieter—almost rhythmic, almost rehearsed.

"Balance must be kept, the cycle must turn,
Light and dark, none shall burn.
Hands that resist will be bound in thread,
Only the willing may walk ahead, Vra ko Nikri."

Liam stiffened. That last part—he had never heard it before. The words sent a strange shiver down his spine, like something buried deep in his mind had been disturbed.

"Nari... where did you hear that?"

She looked at him, confusion flickering across her face. "I... I don't know. It just felt natural to say."

They fell into comfortable silence, the weight of unspoken thoughts settling between them. They had spent years together, fighting side by side, bleeding for each other, saving each other. Their connection ran deeper than words, stronger than orders. It was a bond forged in fire, in battle, in trust that neither of them had ever dared to break.

But something was different tonight. There was a strange unease lingering in the air, a shift in the fabric of their reality that neither of them could quite name.

Nari sighed, rubbing the back of her neck. "I think I'm gonna call it a night. Long day tomorrow."

Liam nodded, watching as she stood up, stretching slightly. "Yeah. Get some rest. I'll see you in the morning."

She offered him a small smile before heading inside, disappearing into the dimly lit hallway that led to her room. Liam stayed on the rooftop a moment longer, watching the city breathe beneath him, unaware that this would be the last night he'd know Nari as she was.

The Transformation

The air in Nari's room was still, heavy with a strange, unplaceable tension. She had fallen asleep quickly, exhaustion from their latest mission pulling her into deep rest. But the peace didn't last.

Something slithered.

A faint movement in the darkness. A whisper of something unnatural.

Her breathing hitched, her body shifting slightly as if sensing the intrusion before her mind did. The shadows in the corner of the room twisted, coalescing into something living, something sentient. Then—

A parasite.

It moved with impossible fluidity, its inky form stretching, shifting, crawling. It found its way to the bed, its tendrils weaving through the air like searching fingers. Then, with a grotesque sort of elegance, it crawled into her nose.

Nari's body jerked. Her eyes snapped open—but they were no longer her own.

A surge of something foreign coursed through her veins, burning like liquid fire. Her muscles spasmed, her hands clutching at the sheets as an unbearable heat spread through her chest, her spine, her skull. It felt like drowning in flames, like being torn apart and stitched back together all at once. A silent scream echoed in her mind, but her lips remained parted in eerie silence.

Then, her pupils dilated. The deep brown of her irises melted away, shifting into a haunting, luminous blue. Not just blue—glowing. Ethereal, otherworldly, unnatural.

Her breathing steadied. Her fingers uncurled.

Slowly, she sat up, tilting her head as if adjusting to the new sensations, the new awareness flooding her mind. The world looked… different. Clearer. Sharper. Every sound was amplified—the hum of electricity in the walls, the faint rustling of the wind against the glass, the rhythmic pulse of her own heartbeat.

She stood, moving toward the mirror across the room. Her reflection stared back at her, familiar yet entirely foreign. The deep blue eyes. The unnaturally smooth, almost porcelain-like skin. The aura of something no longer fully human.

And then, she smiled.

But it wasn't her smile.

It was something else. Something other.

Morning Routine and Meeting at Headquarters

By the time the sun rose, Nari had already showered, dressed, and prepared for the day ahead. She moved through her usual routine—brushing her hair, tying her boots, strapping on her watch—but it all felt different. As if she were operating on instinct rather than thought.

The world had shifted overnight. She could **hear** the city breathing, sense the people moving beyond the walls, feel the pulse of energy coursing through the air. But she remained outwardly composed, her posture relaxed, her expression neutral.

When she stepped into the kitchen, Liam was already there, leaning against the counter with a steaming cup of coffee in hand. His eyes flickered to her as she entered, and for a moment, there was something unreadable in his gaze.

"You're up early," he noted.

Nari smiled—the same smile, yet different. "Figured I'd get a head start."

Liam studied her for a second longer before nodding. "Big day today."

She tilted her head slightly, as if considering his words. "Yeah. Big day."

They left for headquarters soon after, slipping into the sleek black car waiting outside. The ride was quiet, the usual hum of conversation absent. Liam could feel it—the change.

He just didn't know what it meant yet.

At Headquarters.

The intelligence headquarters was as sterile and imposing as ever. Glass walls, reinforced steel, the scent of coffee and tension thick in the air. Agents bustled from one room to the next, locked in hushed conversations, exchanging files and orders like pieces on a chessboard.

Liam and Nari entered side by side, their presence turning heads. But Nari barely noticed. She was listening—not with her ears, but with something deeper. Every conversation, every heartbeat, every flicker of movement felt like it belonged to her, like she was part of the system itself.

Liam didn't speak as they made their way toward the briefing room. His instincts were screaming at him, though he couldn't explain why. He glanced at Nari again, watching the way she moved—calm, graceful, eerily composed.

Something had changed. And he was about to find out what.

Chapter 4:
The Unseen Shift

The hum of activity at intelligence headquarters was nothing unusual—agents moving in and out of secured rooms, hushed voices whispering classified information, the soft clicks of keyboards filling the air. But today, something was different.

Liam noticed it the moment they walked in.

He had spent years memorizing the way Nari moved, the way she carried herself with quiet confidence. But today, there was something *off*. Her footsteps were too measured, her posture too rigid, her gaze just a little too distant. It was subtle, barely noticeable to anyone who didn't know her like he did.

As they entered the main operations room, agents greeted them with nods and brief glances before returning to their work. Nari responded as she always did—calm, professional, unreadable. But Liam caught the hesitation, the fraction-of-a-second delay before she spoke.

She was *thinking* about how to act normal.

And that wasn't like her at all.

A Disquieting Change

Liam sat at his desk, watching as Nari interacted with their colleagues. She was efficient, precise, blending seamlessly into the routine of the agency. But that was the problem—she was *too* seamless. Too perfect.

He noticed the way her eyes flickered across the room, taking in everything at once, scanning people, memorizing patterns of speech, breathing, movement. It was as if she were studying them, analyzing them in real-time.

Then there were the small things. The way she barely blinked. The way she seemed to anticipate conversations before they even happened. The way her fingers drummed against the table in a perfectly rhythmic pattern, like a metronome set at an exact tempo.

And most unsettling of all—

Her smile.

Nari had always been a master of deception. She could lie, infiltrate, manipulate without breaking a sweat. But the way she smiled now—it wasn't natural. It was calculated. Like she was mimicking an emotion rather than feeling it.

Liam exhaled, rubbing his temple. Maybe he was overthinking it. Maybe the exhaustion of their last mission was just catching up with them both.

But deep down, he knew better.

An Unexpected Encounter

During lunch, Liam found himself in the break room with their colleague, Darren Cole, an agent who had been with the organization almost as long as they had. He was mid-sentence about a mission briefing when Nari walked in.

Darren's voice faltered for just a second as he looked at her. His brow furrowed slightly, as if he, too, had sensed something.

"Hey, Nari," Darren greeted, offering her a nod.

She smiled. "Hey, Darren. How's the new assignment?"

Darren hesitated. "Uh… same as always. Lot of recon, a lot of waiting. You know how it is."

Nari's eyes lingered on him for a second longer than necessary before she nodded. "Of course. Same as always."

Liam watched the exchange carefully. Darren was uneasy. The way he shifted slightly in his chair, the way his fingers curled around his coffee cup a little too tightly—it was all too familiar. It was the instinctive reaction of a trained agent sensing something wrong.

But Nari didn't notice. Or if she did, she didn't care.

Liam Investigates

That night, after everyone had cleared out of the main offices, Liam stayed behind. He needed answers.

He accessed the agency's biometric database, running a subtle scan of Nari's recent activity. He wasn't looking for anything obvious—if something had changed about her physically, the system would have flagged it. But he wasn't expecting what he found.

Her vitals were perfect. Too perfect.

Heart rate—steady. Too steady.

Reflex scans—above average. Far above average.

Reaction times—inhumanly precise.

It was as if her body had been *optimized*, refined to its peak without any signs of fatigue, stress, or natural fluctuations.

And then there was the final piece.

A security recording from earlier that morning—Nari entering headquarters. Liam watched as she moved through the halls, greeting agents, acting normal. Then she passed by a security camera and looked straight into it.

For a full five seconds, she stared into the lens, her eyes glowing faintly in the infrared recording.

Then, she smiled.

Liam slammed the laptop shut, his pulse spiking.

Something was wrong. And he was going to find out what.

Chapter 5:
The Dreamland of Truth

The lights in the headquarters flickered slightly as the evening settled in, casting long shadows across the steel-gray walls. Liam and Nari sat in the lounge, a rare moment of quiet between them. Their latest mission had been wrapped up, and for once, there was no immediate briefing, no sudden calls to action—just a moment to exist.

Nari sipped her tea, her expression calm but unreadable. "Feels strange, doesn't it? Having nothing to do."

Liam smirked, leaning back in his chair. "We could enjoy it for once. Maybe even pretend we're normal people."

She chuckled softly, tapping her fingers against the rim of her cup. "If only pretending made it real."

Liam exhales, rubbing his temple.
"You ever wonder if we actually have a choice in all this? Like... what if we were never in control to begin with?"

Nari tilts her head, her eyes unreadable. "What do you mean?"

He shrugs, a strange chill running down his spine. "What if something out there is deciding everything for us? Making us think we're fighting for the right cause, making us think we even want this life."

Silence. Then—

Nari's lips part slightly, but she doesn't answer. Instead, her voice shifts—soft, rhythmic, almost rehearsed.

"Balance must be kept, the cycle must turn...
Light and dark, none shall burn...
Hands that resist will be bound in thread,
Only the willing may walk ahead...
Vra ko Nikri."

Liam stiffens. A strange fog fills his mind, like a pressure wrapping around his thoughts. His vision blurs for a second, refocusing just as Nari lifts her gaze to meet his—her eyes now glowing an unnatural, vibrant green.

Liam barely had a second to react before an unnatural wave of dizziness crashed over him. His vision blurred, the room around him distorting as if reality itself was unraveling. His muscles slackened, his breath caught in his throat, and before he could form a single coherent thought—

The world faded.

The Dreamland

Liam woke to the scent of salt and the sound of crashing waves.

He was standing on the shore of an endless ocean, the sky above painted in hues of deep violet and shimmering gold. The air was thick, almost unreal, carrying a sense of tranquility that didn't belong.

A presence stirred beside him.

Nari.

But not as he knew her.

She stood barefoot on the shore, the water gently lapping at her ankles. She wore a white dress, flowing like mist, and her dark hair cascaded in waves down her back. When she turned to him, her green eyes glowed faintly, the only sign that this wasn't reality.

Liam tried to move, to speak, but his body felt strangely weightless, as if he wasn't fully there.

"This place..." he murmured, his voice distant even to his own ears.

"A dream," Nari answered softly. "But not yours."

Liam's jaw clenched. "What did you do to me?"

She took a step closer, the sand beneath her feet undisturbed. "I needed you to see. To understand."

He forced himself to focus. "Understand what?"

She lifted her hand, and suddenly, the ocean around them shifted.

Images rose from the water's surface—fragments of memories, pieces of truth hidden behind years of deception. Liam saw familiar faces—agents, superiors, people he had trusted. And then he saw what lay beneath.

Corruption.

Orders that weren't about protection but elimination. Missions designed not to save lives, but to control them. Manipulation, false threats, engineered wars—it was all there, unfolding like a carefully crafted illusion.

Liam felt his heart hammering in his chest. "This isn't real. This is just—"

"It is real." Nari's voice was steady, unwavering. "You've just never been allowed to see it."

The weight of it crushed down on him. He had followed orders without question, believing in the greater cause. But what if the cause had never been just? What if they had been the villains all along?

Nari stepped closer, reaching up to touch his temple. The moment her fingers grazed his skin, a final memory surged into his mind—a mission briefing, months ago. The parasite threat. The moment his superiors had first labeled it an "enemy." But in the memory, he saw something else.

The fear in their eyes.

Not fear of destruction, but fear of losing control.

Liam gasped as he stumbled back, the world around him warping, shattering, breaking apart like glass.

The Depths of the Mind

He tumbled backward into darkness, but instead of waking up, he fell into another vision—

A city in flames. Soldiers marching. Civilians silenced, not by force, but by obedience they never questioned.

The organization wasn't protecting them.

It was controlling them.

"You see it now, don't you?" Nari's voice whispered from the void.

Liam turned, but she was everywhere and nowhere at once.

He watched his past replay—missions where civilians disappeared without explanation, where rebels were executed before they could speak, where information was altered to suit the organization's goals. He saw himself—a pawn, blindly following orders.

His stomach twisted. "No... No, that can't be right. We're the good guys. We have to be."

Nari appeared before him again, placing her hand on his chest. "What is 'good' when your choices were never yours?"

A shockwave of energy pulsed from her touch, and suddenly, Liam was standing back in his own memories, but this time, he could feel what had been hidden from him.

The doubt.

The cracks in his loyalty.

Moments where he had felt the truth but had been conditioned to ignore it.

"No," he whispered, his voice breaking. "If this is real, then what am I supposed to do?"

Nari's expression softened. "Wake up."

And then—

The world collapsed.

Awakening

He woke with a sharp inhale, his body jerking upright.

He was back in the lounge. The dim lighting, the faint hum of machinery—it was all as it had been before. But something was different.

Nari sat across from him, perfectly composed, as if nothing had happened. But her eyes—they were brown again.

"Liam?" she asked, tilting her head slightly. "Are you okay?"

His breath was uneven, his pulse racing. He stared at her, trying to reconcile what he had just seen—what he had just felt.

Had it all been in his mind? A hallucination? Or had he truly glimpsed something he was never meant to know?

And if so—

Who was really in control?

Chapter 6:
The Factory's Secret

Liam's heart pounded as he navigated the dimly lit corridors of headquarters. The dream—or vision—Nari had shown him still clung to his mind like a fog that refused to lift. His gut told him to investigate, to dig deeper into the unsettling truth she had revealed. He needed proof.

As he moved past secured doors and empty offices, a thought struck him. There was an old, abandoned factory adjacent to headquarters, a place that had long been deemed useless. He had overheard whispers among agents—something was hidden there, something too important to destroy, yet too dangerous to be left in the open.

His instincts flared. If there was any place to start, it was there.

Into the Shadows

Liam slipped out of the main building and into the cold night air. The factory loomed ahead, a skeletal structure of rusting metal and broken windows. It had once been used for manufacturing, but its original purpose had long been forgotten, left to decay under layers of dust and silence.

The air was thick with the scent of damp metal and decay. The moonlight cast eerie shadows through the shattered windows, creating jagged patterns on the ground. Every step Liam took was deliberate, his muscles tense with anticipation. This place felt wrong—not just abandoned, but deliberately erased from memory.

The front doors were sealed shut with heavy chains, rusted but still sturdy. He tested them—no give. He knew better than to take the obvious route. Circling the perimeter, he searched for an alternate entry. His keen eyes landed on a broken ventilation shaft near the back, just large enough to squeeze through.

He climbed up, pried off the rusted grate, and crawled inside. The metal groaned under his weight, but he moved with practiced silence. The shaft was narrow, the air stale, as if it hadn't been disturbed in years. Each movement sent dust swirling in the dim light. The passage twisted downward before opening into a vast space—

A warehouse, untouched by time.

Machines stood still like forgotten sentinels, conveyor belts hanging limp, their motors lifeless. The floor was littered with broken tools, remnants of a past long buried. It was an industrial graveyard, but something had been left behind.

Then he saw it—a massive table in the center of the room, covered in a thick layer of dust, draped in an old, tattered cloth. The atmosphere was oppressive, untouched by time, as if whatever lay beneath had been waiting for someone to find it.

Liam hesitated. A deep, unsettling feeling clawed at his chest, whispering that once he looked, there would be no turning back.

He reached out, grabbed the cloth, and ripped it away.

The Horrifying Discovery

Underneath the dust and webs, plans.

Liam's breath hitched as his eyes roamed across the pages, pinned in meticulous order. Schematics, calculations, government approvals—all leading to a singular, unthinkable project.

A nuclear missile.

But not just any missile—one aimed at Earth itself.

Liam staggered back, his mind racing. He scanned the documents again, searching for any sign of misinterpretation, but the evidence was undeniable. The organization, the people he had sworn loyalty to, were planning the unthinkable.

Blueprints showed missile silos hidden beneath the surface of major cities. Detailed simulations predicted destruction at a scale beyond anything in recorded history. Documents with official stamps outlined classified operations, confirming high-ranking officials' involvement in the conspiracy.

Why? Who was the target? What could justify this level of destruction?

He turned another page and felt his blood run cold.

Strategic Targets: Major Cities Worldwide.

It wasn't an attack on a singular enemy. It was a global reset.

Each city had a red mark slashed across it—New York, Tokyo, London, Moscow. No distinction between allies and enemies. This wasn't war. This was annihilation.

A leather-bound dossier caught his attention, resting at the edge of the table. He opened it, flipping through notes scrawled in hurried handwriting. The words blurred together in his racing mind, but a single sentence stood out, etched in bold ink:

"We must control the chaos. If we cannot rule the world, we will burn it and start anew."

Liam clenched his fists, his breath ragged. The organization had lied to them all. They had never been protectors. They were puppeteers, controlling the world not through security, but through fear and devastation.

He had to stop this. He had to—

A sudden creak behind him sent his instincts into overdrive.

He whirled around, hand on his weapon, only to be met with darkness. But he wasn't alone. A presence lingered, watching, waiting.

A whisper drifted from the shadows. "You weren't supposed to see that."

Liam's pulse spiked. His cover was blown.

And now, they were coming for him.

A cold wind swept through the factory, rustling the papers, making the documents tremble like whispers of the damned. The air itself seemed to grow heavier, pressing against his chest like an unseen force.

Then—

A shadow moved.

Liam ducked, instincts kicking in a second before a knife embedded itself in the wooden table where his head had just been. He rolled to the side, drawing his firearm, his eyes scanning the darkness.

Another figure emerged, stepping into the dim light—a masked operative, clad in black, their stance poised for a kill.

Liam didn't wait. He fired.

The shot rang out, the echo bouncing off the metal walls. The figure dodged with inhuman speed, vanishing into the maze of rusted beams and broken machinery.

Liam's breath came quick. They knew he was here. And if one was here, there were more.

A voice crackled in his earpiece. Static at first, then—

"Liam, get out of there. Now."

It was Nari.

His grip on his gun tightened. She knew?

"How did you—"

"No time! They're sending reinforcements. You need to leave."

Liam ground his teeth. He had to make a choice—take the files and risk fighting his way out, or run now and return later.

A clang from above made the decision for him. More operatives swarmed into the upper levels of the factory, their red laser sights sweeping through the dark.

Liam grabbed as many documents as he could, stuffing them into his jacket. Then he ran.

The factory became a battleground. Bullets ricocheted off rusted beams. Footsteps pounded against the metal catwalks above. Liam sprinted for the ventilation shaft, dodging between the abandoned machinery.

A bullet grazed his shoulder. He bit down a curse, pain flaring down his arm.

"Left! Take the old conveyor exit!" Nari's voice guided him through the chaos.

He spotted it—an open conveyor belt chute leading outside. No time to hesitate.

Liam dove, sliding down into the dark, tumbling out into the cold night air. He hit the ground rolling, gasping as his wound throbbed.

The factory behind him was now fully awake with enemy forces. They wouldn't stop until he was dead.

Liam forced himself up, clutching the stolen files. He had the proof now. The organization's true intentions.

And now, he was officially a fugitive.

The real fight had just begun.

Chapter 7:
Seven Days of Shadows

The revelation had shaken Liam to his core. The organization he had devoted his life to was orchestrating the unthinkable—a global reset through nuclear destruction. He had the proof now, but proof meant nothing without a plan. He needed to act, but recklessness would only get him killed.

He had seven days before the final activation sequence would begin. Seven days to gather intel, find allies, and uncover the full scope of the conspiracy.

Seven days to stop the end of the world.

Day 1: The First Step into Darkness

Liam didn't sleep that night. The weight of the truth pressed against his skull like an iron vice. Every instinct screamed at him to run, but he couldn't—not yet. His first task was survival. If the organization suspected him, he wouldn't live long enough to make a move.

He returned to headquarters as if nothing had changed. As he walked through the pristine white corridors, the security cameras followed his every move. He could feel the eyes of hidden operatives on him. They were always watching, always listening.

His first move was subtle—a test.

He walked into the intelligence archives, where mission records were stored under layers of encryption. His clearance allowed him access to many files, but now he was searching for something buried. Something even he wasn't meant to see.

Using his credentials, he searched for the term: Project Iron Dawn.

ACCESS DENIED.

A second attempt. A different approach.

ACCESS DENIED.

His heart pounded. This was worse than he thought. Even within the highest ranks, information about the nuclear strike was locked away. He needed a backdoor.

The moment he left the archives, he noticed something. A shadow lingering in his periphery. Someone had been watching him.

He turned a corner quickly, cutting through one of the maintenance corridors, and pressed himself against the cold metal wall. Footsteps followed. They were deliberate. Measured.

Not a coincidence.

A tail.

Liam forced himself to breathe evenly. He needed to play this smart. No sudden movements. No panic.

He resumed walking at a normal pace, pretending not to notice. But now, he was on alert. He took a detour to the lower levels of headquarters, where the older security cameras had blind spots. If someone was following him, he needed to confirm it.

A reflection in a glass door ahead of him showed a man in a dark suit, keeping his distance but matching Liam's pace. The tail wasn't even trying to hide. That meant one thing—the organization already suspected him.

Liam entered an empty break room, waiting behind the door. As soon as the tail walked in, Liam struck. He grabbed the man by the collar, slammed him into the wall, and pressed a knife to his throat.

"Why are you following me?" Liam growled.

The agent smirked. "You've been asking the wrong questions, Liam."

Liam's grip tightened. "What do you know?"

The agent didn't answer. He just smiled—a knowing, eerie grin. A second later, he bit down hard on something in his mouth.

Cyanide.

Liam pulled back in horror as the agent collapsed, foam bubbling at his lips. The body twitched once, then went still.

The organization had sent a disposable spy after him.

The message was clear: They knew. And they would rather kill their own than let Liam uncover the truth.

He wiped his knife clean, his pulse hammering. If he had any doubts before, they were gone now.

He was officially a target.

Day 2: The Whisper Network

Liam's next move was finding the cracks in the organization's armor. No system was perfect. Someone, somewhere, had to know **something.**

The lower-level analysts were oblivious—brainwashed by false intelligence. But the field operatives? The ones who had been on the ground, executing orders without question? They had seen too much.

Liam approached **Agent Reynolds**, a seasoned operative with a reputation for loose lips after a few drinks. Reynolds had been part of **Operation Scorched Veil**, a mission classified at the same level as **Iron Dawn.**

Over whiskey in a dimly lit bar, Liam pressed him for details.

"Scorched Veil?" Reynolds chuckled, shaking his head. "You don't want to dig into that, man."

"Humor me."

Reynolds hesitated, then leaned in. "Ever hear about the population control protocols? The failsafes? Let's just say... not every war we fought was necessary. Some were **designed.** You think we're protecting the world? We're **trimming it.**"

Liam's fingers tightened around his glass. He had suspected as much, but hearing it confirmed sent a chill through his spine.

"And Iron Dawn?" Liam asked.

Reynolds' smile vanished. "Don't ask about that one. I don't want to disappear."

Liam had what he needed. A breadcrumb—but one that led deeper down the abyss.

He left the bar with his mind racing. **If they were trimming the world, Iron Dawn wasn't just an operation. It was a purge.**

And he was running out of time.

Day 3: Ghosts in the Machine

Liam knew that accessing restricted files through conventional means was impossible. But he had an ace—Nari.

Since her transformation, she had become... different. More precise. More efficient. But she wasn't fully controlled. Not yet.

"I need your help," he said, catching her in the empty corridor outside the briefing room.

She regarded him with cool, unreadable eyes. "With what?"

"I need access to something hidden. Something they don't want us to see."

For a moment, she simply stared at him. Then, without a word, she turned and led him to the data center.

Her hands moved across the console with inhuman speed. Firewalls collapsed. Encryptions unraveled. She wasn't just hacking the system—she was bending it to her will.

The screen flashed.

PROJECT IRON DAWN.

The files opened.

Liam barely had time to skim before red warning signs flashed across the screen—

Security breach detected.

"GO!" Nari hissed, shoving him toward the exit. "I'll cover you."

Liam ran.

The first alarm had been triggered. The hunt was beginning.

Day 4: The Assassin's Trail

Liam was being hunted.

After the security breach, the organization had deployed cleaners—elite assassins trained to erase problems before they escalated. Their methods were brutal, swift, and absolute.

He couldn't go back to headquarters. Instead, he moved through the city's underground, using abandoned tunnels and black-market safe houses. He needed to throw his pursuers off his trail.

But they found him first.

Liam had just entered an old subway tunnel when he heard it—a sharp intake of breath behind him. Instinct kicked in. He spun, just as a blade sliced through the air where his throat had been.

The assassin moved like a phantom, dressed in tactical gear, his face obscured by a black mask. No words. No hesitation. Just pure intent to kill.

Liam barely blocked the next attack, twisting to avoid a knife to the ribs. He countered, landing a brutal elbow to the assassin's throat. The man staggered but didn't fall. These weren't regular killers—they were trained for one thing: eliminating traitors.

Another figure dropped from the ceiling. More of them. He was outnumbered.

Liam dodged another strike, then disarmed the first assassin in a flash. He plunged the stolen knife into the man's chest and spun, grabbing the wrist of the second assassin before he could fire his silenced pistol.

A gunshot rang out—

Not from the enemy.

One of the assassins froze in mid-motion, his pistol slipping from his fingers as his eyes glowed blue. He turned, expression blank, and without hesitation, fired upon his own teammates.

Liam's pulse hammered. He turned—

Nari was floating above them.

She was different. Ethereal. Powerful.

Her dark hair drifted unnaturally as if caught in an invisible current. Her pale skin almost glowed against the dim tunnel lights. And her eyes—unnervingly bright—stared blankly at the assassins.

Liam took an instinctive step back. "Nari…?"

The remaining assassins hesitated. They had prepared for Liam—not this. Not her.

Big mistake.

Nari raised a hand, and the air itself seemed to ripple.

One of the assassins staggered, his body lifting off the ground as if invisible wires had wrapped around him. His legs kicked helplessly, eyes wide in terror. Then, with a flick of her wrist—

He was thrown across the tunnel, crashing into a steel beam.

The last assassin tried to flee. Nari barely glanced at him.

His limbs locked mid-run. He let out a strangled gasp, clutching his head, as if something inside was tearing apart his mind. Then—

Snap.

His body went limp before crumpling to the ground.

Silence.

Liam's grip on his knife tightened. His heart was still racing from the fight, but now something else chilled him—fear.

"They were going to kill you," Nari said, her voice eerily calm. "I stopped them."

Liam swallowed hard. "You... you just controlled their minds. How long have you been able to do that?"

Her glowing gaze flickered slightly, as if something deep inside her was trying to resurface. "Since the parasite. And I can do a lot more."

She turned and, without hesitation, lifted off the ground again. Her movement was fluid, effortless—like flying had always been a part of her.

"We need to go," she said.

Liam hesitated. He looked at the lifeless bodies, the way they had no chance against her. This wasn't just an enhancement. This was something entirely different. Something beyond human.

"Where?" he finally asked, gripping his weapon tighter. "They'll be looking for us everywhere."

Nari's eyes flickered again, as if something deeper inside her was processing information at an unnatural speed. The parasite inside her wasn't just making her stronger—it was making her think differently.

"There's an abandoned safehouse in the industrial district," she finally said. "But we need to move now."

Liam nodded, stepping forward. But just as they turned to leave, a faint beeping sound echoed in the tunnel.

His stomach dropped.

A remote-detonated explosive.

Liam grabbed Nari's wrist and ran. "MOVE!"

They sprinted down the tunnel as the first explosion ripped through the underground. Dust and fire shot through the air, collapsing steel beams and concrete around them. The force nearly knocked them off their feet, but Nari—still floating—grabbed Liam's collar and lifted him into the air.

For a moment, they soared over the collapsing tunnel as debris crashed below them.

Liam barely had time to register what was happening before they landed on a catwalk above the tracks. The air was thick with dust and smoke.

"That was close," he muttered, coughing.

Nari remained expressionless, lowering herself back to the ground. "They were waiting for us to take the bait. They'll send more. We need to disappear."

Liam studied her, watching the way she hovered so naturally, her eyes still not entirely human. He had spent years training to be the best, yet in one night, Nari had become something far beyond his level.

And he had no idea if that was a good thing or a bad thing.

The sound of shifting rubble behind them made Liam tense. He turned sharply, knife in hand, expecting another attack—but the only movement came from the settling debris.

His pulse refused to slow.

"Come on," Nari said, starting toward the exit. "We don't have much time."

Liam hesitated for half a second before following. His boots crunched against shattered glass and twisted metal. The acrid stench of burnt insulation filled the air. The tunnel's once dim lights flickered weakly, casting eerie shadows that stretched and twisted along the walls.

Every step forward felt like walking into a new nightmare.

Nari moved ahead, gliding rather than walking, her hair swaying unnaturally even in the still air. Liam had to force himself to keep his focus on the mission—not on how alien she was becoming.

"What if they track us?" he asked.

"They will," Nari admitted, her voice eerily detached. "But they won't find us."

Liam narrowed his eyes. "Why not?"

She turned back, offering him the smallest hint of a smile. "Because I won't let them."

Her eyes flickered blue again, and Liam realized—whatever part of Nari was still human, it was slipping further away.

He kept walking.

Whatever had happened to Nari, whatever she had become—

She wasn't just powerful.

She was terrifying.

And deep down, he wasn't sure if he was looking at his greatest ally—

Or his greatest threat.

Day 5: The Firewall of Deception

Liam had erased himself from the system. Officially, he was dead. But that wouldn't stop the organization from hunting him down. If anything, it made him an even bigger target.

He and Nari lay low in an abandoned industrial warehouse on the outskirts of the city. The walls were covered in rust, the air thick with the scent of oil and decay. It was the kind of place no one wanted to enter unless they had to.

Liam sat on the cold concrete floor, staring at the dim glow of his tablet. The data he had stolen from the organization was encrypted beyond belief, but there had to be a way in. His mind raced as he traced through layers of false information, hidden codes, and fragmented files.

"They knew someone would try to crack this," he muttered.

Nari, who had been hovering near the broken window, turned to him. "Then they knew someone like you existed. That's why they sent assassins."

Liam glanced up at her, noting the way she floated rather than stood. It still unsettled him. Whatever the parasite had done to her, it had changed more than just her abilities—it had altered the way she carried herself, the way she thought.

"You're handling this too well," he said, eyes narrowing.

Nari tilted her head slightly, as if processing his words like a machine would. "I accept my reality."

Liam didn't reply. Instead, he went back to work, typing furiously into the tablet. Minutes stretched into hours. The code was relentless, shifting patterns every few minutes as if it were alive, adapting to his methods.

But Liam wasn't alone in this. He had planned ahead.

He pulled out an old burner phone and dialed a number he hadn't used in years. It rang twice before a voice answered, dripping with amusement.

"Liam Cross. Thought you were dead."

"I need your help, Lucius."

Lucius Grimm—a cybercriminal and one of the best hackers Liam had ever worked with. He was unpredictable, eccentric, and had a grudge against the organization that rivaled Liam's own.

"I don't work for free, you know," Lucius said. "And considering you're supposed to be dead, I assume this is urgent."

"I need to break into the deepest levels of the organization's network. They're running an encrypted operation—Project Iron Dawn. It's bad, Lucius. Nuclear bad."

There was a pause on the other end. Then, a quiet chuckle. "You always get yourself into the best kind of trouble, don't you? Fine. I'll bite. Send me what you have."

Liam forwarded the data he had managed to extract so far. Within moments, Lucius was typing furiously on his end.

"Damn. They weren't kidding about their security. This thing's wrapped in enough layers to make a Russian nesting doll jealous."

"Can you crack it?"

"Can I? Please. It's insulting you even asked. Give me a few minutes."

Liam exhaled, tapping his fingers against the table. He wasn't used to waiting, especially when the stakes were this high. He glanced at Nari, who had been silent during the exchange. Her eyes were locked onto the screen, but she wasn't reading the data—she was watching him.

"What?" Liam asked.

"You trust him?"

Liam hesitated, then nodded. "Lucius may be a criminal, but he hates the organization more than I do. That makes him reliable—at least for now."

Another minute passed. Then—

"Alright, got something," Lucius announced. "You weren't kidding. Iron Dawn isn't just a nuclear program—it's a failsafe. If the organization ever faces total collapse, they'll trigger a global catastrophe to ensure no one can rise against them. It's their way of keeping control, even in death."

Liam's stomach turned. "Tell me you can shut it down."

Lucius let out a whistle. "Easier said than done. There's a physical launch mechanism. I can delay the systems remotely, but to stop it completely, you'll need to be there in person."

Liam clenched his jaw. He had expected as much. "Where's the launch site?"

Lucius was silent for a moment. Then, he sighed. "You're not going to like this."

A map appeared on Liam's screen. His blood ran cold.

The launch site was underground—directly beneath organization headquarters.

"You're telling me we have to walk into the most secure building on the planet and stop a doomsday device?" Liam muttered.

"Pretty much."

Liam turned to Nari. "We have to move. Now."

"Where?"

"To the launch site. If we don't stop this, there won't be a world left to fight for."

Nari stared at him for a long moment. Then, with a slow, deliberate motion, she extended her hand.

"Then we fight."

Liam clasped it without hesitation. For better or worse, they were in this together.

Lucius' voice crackled through the phone one last time. "Good luck, Cross. You're going to need it."

The countdown had begun.

Day 6: A Night at the Club

Liam knew the best way to break an empire wasn't always through brute force—it was through its weakest link. And in this case, that link was Sebastian Vale, the reckless, overindulgent nephew of the CEO.

Sebastian was everything a powerful organization didn't want representing them—a spoiled heir who enjoyed spending nights drowning in alcohol and bad decisions, shielded only by his family's influence. He wasn't directly involved in Project Iron Dawn, but Liam was willing to bet that the man had heard whispers of things he shouldn't have.

And whispers could lead to answers.

The club, Eclipse, was an exclusive underground haven for the elite—dimly lit, pulsing with music, and drowning in an intoxicating mixture of wealth and sin. A place where secrets were spilled between sips of overpriced whiskey and whispered promises.

Liam leaned against the bar, adjusting the silky fabric of the deep red dress he wore. The disguise had been tricky—a blonde wig, subtle makeup, and enough elegance to make the transformation believable. Years of spy work had taught him that people saw what they expected to see. And right now, Sebastian Vale was expecting company.

From across the room, Vale was draped over a velvet lounge chair, his glass half-full, his grin lazy, and his mind already slipping into intoxication. His suit was slightly disheveled, his tie loose. He was surrounded by women—but his wandering eyes meant he was still looking for something more.

Liam smirked.

Time to give him what he wanted.

He moved through the crowd, letting the ambient energy of the club pull him toward his target. As he approached, Sebastian's gaze locked onto him, the hint of a smirk curling on his lips.

"Well, aren't you a sight," Sebastian slurred, lifting his glass in a lazy toast.

Liam laughed lightly, playing the part. "Aren't I just?" He slid into the seat beside him, crossing his legs slowly. "You look like you could use some company."

Sebastian grinned, pleased. "Always. What's your name, darling?"

Liam tilted his head, feigning thought. "Let's keep things... mysterious. Makes the night more interesting, don't you think?"

Sebastian chuckled, drinking deeply. "I like the way you think."

Step one: Engage. Done.

Liam let his fingers dance along the rim of his untouched drink, watching as Sebastian downed another. The man was already half-gone, and that worked in Liam's favor.

"You must be someone important to be here," Liam purred, leaning in slightly. "Or at least connected."

Sebastian grinned smugly. "You could say that."

Liam played coy. "Oh?"

"My uncle practically runs the world," Sebastian said with a drunken chuckle. "I'm part of an empire, sweetheart. Bigger than you could ever imagine."

Liam feigned awe, eyes widening. "An empire? That sounds... powerful. Dangerous."

Sebastian leaned closer, dropping his voice to a conspiratorial whisper. "It is. And it's about to get a lot more powerful."

Liam felt a spark of satisfaction—he was getting somewhere.

"Tell me more," Liam murmured, brushing a delicate touch against Sebastian's arm. "I love powerful men."

Sebastian exhaled, pleased. "Let's just say my uncle has a final solution for dealing with threats. A plan so secure, so unstoppable, that no one will be able to challenge us ever again."

Liam's pulse quickened. This was it.

He let out a breathy laugh, playing into the moment. "That sounds thrilling. But what if someone tried? Surely there's a weakness?"

Sebastian smirked. "No weaknesses. Everything's locked down. But even if someone got close… well, let's just say the launch key isn't where they'd expect it to be."

Liam's mind raced. Launch key.

This was what he needed. "Where is it, then?" he asked, feigning drunken curiosity.

Sebastian laughed, shaking his head. "I probably shouldn't tell you that, huh?"

Liam pouted, running a finger along his jaw. "Oh, but now you've got me curious..."

Sebastian exhaled heavily, shaking his head. The alcohol was doing its job, loosening his tongue. One more push.

Liam leaned in, pressing a whisper against his ear. "You can tell me... just between us."

Sebastian hesitated. Then, with a slow, indulgent grin, he exhaled a single phrase.

"It's inside a vault... beneath headquarters."

Liam hid his triumph beneath a playful smile. "Mmm, that sounds... intriguing."

But before he could push further, Sebastian suddenly squinted at him, tilting his head. His instincts were kicking in.

"Hey, wait a minute... have we met before?" Sebastian mumbled, eyes narrowing.

Liam's heart pounded.

"No," he said smoothly, placing a hand on Sebastian's chest, tilting his head as if playfully offended. "And I thought we were having such a good time."

Sebastian's grin returned, his suspicions melting under intoxication and ego. "We are, we are. Another drink?"

Liam smiled. "Actually, I think I've got everything I need from you."

Before Sebastian could react, Liam drove a tranquilizer into his side.

Sebastian's body stiffened, his pupils dilating in confusion. "Wha—"

His head slumped forward onto the table, completely unconscious.

Liam stood, straightening his dress and adjusting the blonde wig. Mission complete.

Now, he had the final piece of the puzzle. The launch key was inside a vault beneath headquarters.

As he exited the club, Nari was waiting outside in the shadows.

"Did you get it?" she asked, her voice cool and detached.

Liam nodded. "We know where the key is."

Nari's eyes flickered blue. "Then it's time to finish this."

Tomorrow would be the final move.

The endgame had begun.

Day 7: The Turn of Mind

Liam had everything he needed. The launch key was hidden beneath headquarters, and the organization was running out of time. But there was one obstacle left—the Lady Boss.

She was ruthless, intelligent, and unshaken by threats. If there was one person who could still stop him, it was her.

And that was why he needed to turn the tables first.

Liam entered the headquarters through an underground maintenance tunnel. Nari stayed outside, waiting for the right moment to make her move. This was Liam's fight—his final confrontation before reaching the vault.

As he emerged into the dimly lit corridors, his footsteps echoed against the marble flooring. He had disabled the security cameras earlier that morning, giving him a small window of invisibility.

The Lady Boss's office was on the highest floor, a symbol of her dominance over everyone below. Getting there wouldn't be easy.

He slipped into an elevator and pressed the button for the executive floor. His heart pounded with every second. This was it.

The doors opened, revealing an office drenched in opulence—dark wood, gold trimmings, and the scent of expensive cigars lingering in the air. Behind a massive desk, sipping a glass of wine, sat the Lady Boss.

She didn't look surprised to see him.

"Liam Cross," she mused, swirling the wine in her glass. "I must say, I didn't expect you to make it this far."

Liam stepped forward, his muscles coiled for action. "I know everything. Project Iron Dawn. The nuclear failsafe. The vault beneath this building. It ends today."

The Lady Boss exhaled, setting down her glass. "You still think you're the hero, don't you? That you're stopping some great evil. But Liam..." she leaned forward, her piercing gaze locking onto his, "what if I told you that you're wrong?"

Liam frowned. "I don't have time for your mind games."

She smirked. "Oh, but I do."

Before he could react, she whipped out a sleek, silver pistol and fired.

Liam's instincts took over. He twisted sharply, dodging the bullet—but it wasn't a bullet.

A tiny, metallic insect-like device shot past him, barely missing his neck. The moment it hit the wall, its legs twitched and curled inward.

His stomach dropped. A brainwashing bug.

Liam barely had a second to react before she fired another. This time, he was ready.

He lunged, snatching the bug out of the air mid-flight.

The Lady Boss's smirk faltered. "Impossible."

Liam felt the tiny machine squirm between his fingers, its needle-like appendages seeking flesh to burrow into. In one swift motion, he turned and flung it straight back at her.

The bug latched onto the side of her neck.

She gasped, hands flying up to rip it off, but it was too late.

The moment the bug punctured her skin, her pupils dilated. Her breath hitched. Her body trembled.

"N-no..." she whispered, stumbling backward. "I... control... this..."

Liam watched as the iron walls around her mind began to crumble.

She let out a strangled gasp, her knees buckling. Her lips parted as if she wanted to scream, but no sound came out.

Liam's voice dropped to a whisper. "Now you understand what it feels like. To have something else inside your head. To be powerless."

Her hands shook violently as she tried to resist. But resistance was futile.

Her shoulders relaxed. Her breathing slowed. Her resistance shattered.

She blinked once. Twice. And when her gaze met his again—

It was empty.

Liam took a slow breath. "Tell me where the launch key is."

The Lady Boss nodded obediently. "It's beneath the war room. A biometric vault. Only two people have access."

Liam smirked. "And one of them just joined my side."

He gestured toward the door. "Lead the way."

Without hesitation, she turned and walked.

Liam followed, his heart pounding.

The game had changed. The organization's most ruthless leader was now under his control.

And soon, the entire system would fall.

Chapter 8:
Captured in the Shadows

Darkness.

Then a sharp sting at the side of his neck.

Liam gasped as his body jerked awake, his limbs cold and sluggish. His mind struggled to catch up, his vision swimming as he tried to piece together what had happened.

One moment, he had won. The Lady Boss was under his control. He was on the verge of reaching the vault.

Then—a dart.

A sharp pain had exploded at the base of his neck, and then—

Blackness.

Now, he was awake again—but he wished he wasn't.

His wrists and ankles were bound to a metal chair, tight restraints cutting into his skin. The air was thick with the scent of gasoline and metal. The dim, flickering light overhead revealed a grim, industrial space—an abandoned garage, if he had to guess.

In front of him stood two men.

One he knew too well—the CEO. Cold, calculating, a man whose presence alone commanded authority. Stanley Vale.

And beside him—Darren. Liam's former best friend.

Darren's expression was unreadable, but Liam saw the flicker of hesitation in his eyes. Good. He wasn't entirely gone yet.

The CEO stepped forward, clasping his hands behind his back. "Liam Cross. Alive and still full of defiance. I must say, I'm impressed."

Liam smirked despite the pounding in his skull. "Wish I could say the same, Stanley. But you always had that annoying habit of ruining my day."

The CEO chuckled. "Always with the jokes. But tell me, Liam—what exactly do you think you've accomplished? You fought well, I'll give you that. You even managed to outplay the Lady Boss. But did you really think you could win?"

Liam shifted in his chair, testing the restraints. No give. They weren't taking any chances.

"I think I got pretty close," Liam muttered. "And I'm guessing you're not here to congratulate me. So go on, let's skip the speech and get to the part where you start threatening me."

The CEO sighed. "You're always so eager to make things difficult." He nodded toward Darren.

Without hesitation, Darren stepped forward and delivered a brutal punch to Liam's gut.

Liam grunted, his body lurching forward against the restraints. He coughed, trying to catch his breath. So, it was going to be like that.

The CEO leaned in, his voice smooth. "You don't have to suffer, Liam. You don't have to die. All you have to do—is say yes."

Liam exhaled sharply. "To what?"

The CEO smiled. "To coming back home. To working for us again. You were our best. You still can be. This… rebellion of yours? It's nothing more than a mistake. One I'm willing to overlook."

Liam chuckled darkly. "You want me to work for you? After everything? After trying to kill me?"

"You think I wouldn't forgive you?" the CEO mused. "I forgive everything, Liam. Because I know what's best for you."

Liam clenched his jaw. "Yeah? And if I say no?"

The CEO's smile didn't falter. "Then I'm afraid I'll have to let Darren convince you otherwise."

Darren's fists tightened. His eyes flickered with something—guilt? Regret? Liam wasn't sure.

The CEO turned away slightly, speaking in a casual tone. "You see, Liam, you were never meant to be against us. You were meant to be great. But something poisoned you. That girl—Nari."

Liam's fingers twitched. They wanted her, too.

The CEO sighed. "She made you weak. But we can fix that. We can make you stronger."

He turned back toward Liam, reaching into his coat pocket. He pulled out something small, metallic, and familiar.

A brainwashing bug.

Liam's breath hitched.

"You see," the CEO continued, "you're not the first to resist. And you won't be the last. But the thing about the mind, Liam… is that it's fragile. All it takes is a little push in the right direction."

He tossed the bug to Darren.

"Make him one of us again."

Darren hesitated, looking down at the small mechanical device in his palm. His grip tightened.

Liam saw his chance.

"Darren," Liam said, his voice low but firm. "You don't have to do this. You know me. You know who I am. You know who you are."

Darren flinched. The crack in his armor widened.

The CEO narrowed his eyes. "Darren. Now."

Liam locked eyes with his old friend. "You don't want to do this. They took everything from us. They turned us into killers. Do you really think they'll let you go if you do this? You'll just be another puppet. Just like they wanted."

Darren's breathing grew heavy. His hand shook.

"Darren!" the CEO snapped. "Do it!"

And then—

Darren turned sharply—and threw the bug at the CEO instead.

The CEO's eyes widened, but he was too slow.

The bug latched onto his neck. It burrowed into his skin.

The CEO choked, his body going rigid. His pupils dilated. His mouth opened slightly, as if trying to speak—but no words came.

Silence filled the garage.

Then, in an eerily calm voice, the CEO whispered his own command.

"Release Liam."

The guards obeyed without hesitation, unlocking his restraints.

Liam sprang to his feet.

He turned to Darren, who was still frozen, hands shaking from what he had just done.

"You made the right choice," Liam said, clapping him on the shoulder.

Darren exhaled, nodding. "Let's finish this."

Liam turned back to the CEO, whose vacant stare was now awaiting his next order.

Liam smirked. "Tell me how to get into the vault."

The CEO blinked once. "Biometric scan. My palm. Only I can open it."

Liam grinned. "Perfect. Let's go."

The final battle was about to begin.

Chapter 9:
The Final Stand

The cold steel of the underground bunker sent a shiver up Liam's spine. The air was thick with the scent of oil, sweat, and imminent destruction.

The moment Liam and Darren stepped toward the missile chamber, the alarm system screeched to life.

A dozen heavily armed guards stormed the corridor, rifles raised.

Liam barely had time to react before the first shot whizzed past his ear, embedding itself in the metal wall beside him. The explosion of gunfire sent shockwaves through the hall, forcing Liam and Darren to dive for cover behind a thick concrete column.

"They were waiting for us!" Darren shouted, loading his pistol with shaking hands.

Liam peeked around the corner, his sharp eyes analyzing their formation. Four guards in front, three covering the left flank, another three pressing in from behind. The remaining two were standing by the reinforced steel doors, protecting what lay beyond—the nuclear missile.

Their last chance to stop the apocalypse.

"We push forward," Liam decided, gripping his silencer tightly. "We don't have time for a firefight."

Darren exhaled sharply, nodding. "Then we make every bullet count."

Liam swung out first, firing two precise shots. One guard collapsed immediately, a bullet between his eyes. The other staggered, clutching his throat before hitting the ground.

Darren moved next, rolling across the floor and firing a series of quick bursts. Two guards fell, their weapons clattering against the concrete.

But the others were ready.

One of the guards hurled a flashbang.

"Close your eyes!" Liam barked, just before the grenade detonated.

Even with his eyes shut, the searing white light burned through his eyelids, leaving him momentarily stunned. His ears rang violently, muffling the world around him.

When his vision returned, a guard was already on him.

The brute lunged, swinging a baton straight for Liam's head. Liam ducked, dodging the lethal strike by mere inches. He retaliated with a quick jab to the ribs, but the guard barely flinched—armored vest.

The guard swung again. This time, Liam caught his wrist mid-air and twisted, forcing the weapon from his hand. With a sharp spin, he delivered a devastating kick to the man's knee, sending him crashing down.

Snap.

The guard screamed as his leg buckled in the wrong direction.

Darren, meanwhile, grappled with another attacker. He threw an elbow into the guard's stomach, then slammed his gun across the man's face, knocking him unconscious.

They had cleared half the room.

But then—the final door guards lifted their automatic rifles.

Liam's heart slammed against his ribs.

"DOWN!" he roared.

Bullets ripped through the air. Sparks and debris exploded from the walls. The noise was deafening, each gunshot reverberating through the tight space like a thunderclap.

Liam and Darren scrambled for cover, barely avoiding the onslaught.

But they were running out of time. They had to end this now.

Liam's eyes darted across the room—then he saw it.

An overhead industrial crane suspended a steel container right above the guards.

It was risky.

It was reckless.

But it was their only shot.

"Cover me!" Liam shouted as he sprinted toward the control panel on the far wall.

Darren laid down suppressive fire, forcing the remaining guards to stay pinned. Liam vaulted over debris, bullets barely missing him, until he reached the panel. His fingers flew over the controls.

With a metallic groan, the crane lurched forward.

The guards realized too late.

The steel container plummeted from above, slamming onto the final two guards with a sickening CRASH.

Silence.

Then—the doors to the missile chamber hissed open.

Liam and Darren stumbled inside, breathing heavily. The room was massive, lined with glowing control panels and towering metal structures. But none of it mattered.

What mattered was the missile.

It stood at the heart of the chamber—a mechanical behemoth primed for destruction.

And the countdown had begun.

00:02:43

Liam's blood ran cold. "It's armed. We have less than three minutes."

Darren rushed to the nearest console. "Can you shut it down?!"

Liam's fingers flew across the keyboard, searching for a manual override.

ACCESS DENIED.

His heart pounded. "It's encrypted. There's no way to disable it from here."

Darren's face paled. "Then how do we stop it?!"

Liam's eyes darted to the base of the missile.

"We blow it up."

Darren blinked. "Blow up a nuclear warhead?! Are you insane?!"

"We don't have a choice!" Liam pulled a small detonator charge from his vest. "A controlled explosion will disable the launch sequence. It won't detonate the warhead itself."

Darren swallowed hard. "That's a lot of trust in 'controlled.'"

00:01:37

Liam sprinted to the base of the missile, planting the explosives along the critical support beams. His hands were steady, despite the roaring chaos in his mind.

Darren covered him, watching the door. "I hope you know what you're doing."

00:00:58

Liam pressed the final button. "Get back!"

They sprinted behind a blast shield.

Liam pressed the trigger.

BOOM.

The explosion ripped through the missile's core.

The ground shook violently. Metal groaned and twisted, the force of the blast tearing the launch mechanism apart. Sparks rained from above as the entire system collapsed in on itself.

But something was wrong.

The shockwave was stronger than expected. The explosion was spreading.

A second blast wave erupted, hurling Liam and Darren across the chamber.

Liam crashed into the floor, his body screaming in pain. His vision blurred. The world tilted.

Somewhere in the distance, Darren groaned.

Liam tried to stand, but his legs gave out. Blood dripped from a deep gash in his forehead, staining his vision red.

He forced himself to crawl.

Darren.

He saw him lying near the wreckage, barely moving. Smoke and fire flickered around them.

Liam dragged himself forward, each movement agony.

"Darren—"

His voice caught in his throat.

Darren's chest barely rose. Blood pooled beneath him.

A piece of shrapnel was lodged deep in his side.

Liam's stomach twisted. No. No, not like this.

He grabbed Darren's hand. It was cold.

Darren's lips moved, barely a whisper. "Liam… did we win?"

Liam nodded furiously, even as his vision blurred with unshed tears. "Yeah. We did. It's over."

Darren exhaled a shaky breath. "Good… that's good."

His fingers tightened for a moment, then slowly loosened.

And then—

Darren went still.

Liam froze.

The sounds of the burning wreckage faded into nothing.

And in that moment—

Liam had won. But he had lost everything.

Chapter 10:
The Revelation

Darkness loomed over the ruins of the underground facility. Smoke curled into the air, rising from the wreckage of what had once been the missile chamber. The echoes of the explosion still rang in Liam's ears as he knelt beside Darren's lifeless body, the weight of loss pressing down on him like an unbearable force.

Blood pooled beneath Darren, a cruel reminder of the sacrifice he had made. Liam's fingers trembled as he reached out, closing his fallen friend's vacant eyes. He swallowed the grief, forcing himself to stand, even as his legs threatened to give out beneath him. There was no time to mourn—not yet.

Then, the temperature in the room shifted.

A strange presence prickled at the back of Liam's mind, sending a chill down his spine. The air thickened, the shadows along the walls twisting unnaturally.

And then—

They appeared.

A figure emerged from the darkness, their form shifting, pulsating as if they were not fully bound to this reality. Their features were almost human—but wrong. Their eyes gleamed like twin sapphires, glowing in the dim light, their expression unreadable.

More figures stepped forward, their movements unnaturally fluid. They were tall, elegant yet eerie, their bodies wrapped in dark, armor-like skin. Their fingers were long and clawed, but their presence wasn't hostile.

Liam staggered back, his breath hitching. He had seen monsters. He had fought demons in human skin. But these—these were something else entirely.

One of them, the tallest among them, stepped forward. His voice was deep, resonant, vibrating in Liam's bones.

"You have done well, Liam Cross."

Liam's heart pounded. His body screamed at him to move, to run—but he stood his ground. "Who... who are you?"

The figure tilted his head slightly. "We are the balance keepers. The remnants of a lost world. We are the ones who have been watching."

Liam's fingers twitched toward his weapon, but he hesitated. "Watching? Watching what?"

"Everything."

Another figure spoke, her voice smooth like silk, yet cold as ice. "You were chosen, Liam. You and Nari."

Liam's breath caught at the mention of her name. "Where is she? What have you done to her?"

The lead figure's eyes narrowed slightly. "We have not harmed her. She is… one of us now."

Liam's pulse skyrocketed. "The hell does that mean?"

The alien-like being stepped closer, his movement unnervingly smooth. "You have questions. We will answer them. But first—you must understand."

Liam clenched his fists. "Understand what? That you hijack people's bodies? That you turn them into… into what? Mindless slaves?"

The being's eyes flickered. "Is that what you believe?"

Liam held his ground. "I know what I've seen. Nari—she wasn't the same. Her eyes, her voice—she changed. That wasn't her anymore."

A pause. Then, the being exhaled slowly, his shoulders shifting ever so slightly. "She has not changed, Liam. She has evolved."

Liam narrowed his eyes. "That sounds like the same thing."

The female parasite stepped forward now, her features delicate yet unnatural. "You misunderstand what we are. We do not erase. We do not consume. We empower. We bring clarity."

Liam scoffed. "By forcing people into it? Sounds a lot like control to me."

The leader of the parasites stepped forward, his gaze piercing through Liam. "Do you not feel it? Even now, you are fighting something greater than yourself. The pain, the loss—it consumes you. It weakens you. What if you could cast it away?"

Liam's hands clenched. "And let you take over? No thanks."

The parasite studied him for a long moment. "You believe you have won. That you have stopped the missile, saved your world. But tell me—what have you truly won? You stand among ruin, drenched in the blood of a man who fought beside you. And what awaits you when you leave this place? A world that will never know your sacrifice? A life where the pain will never fade?"

Liam took a step back, his breath uneven. "You're trying to manipulate me."

The female parasite's voice was softer, almost soothing. "We are offering you freedom."

"Freedom?" Liam spat. "By what? Letting you crawl into my mind?"

"Freedom from suffering. Freedom from regret."

Liam's breathing was heavy. His body ached, his mind burned with exhaustion. And deep down, in the place he never wanted to admit existed—he knew they were right.

The pain wouldn't fade.

The guilt wouldn't disappear.

He would live every day remembering Darren's sacrifice, remembering what it cost to survive.

"Liam," the leader said, his voice gentler now. "You believe yourself whole, but you are fractured. You believe yourself strong, but you are bound by your past. We do not take. We restore."

Liam's hands shook. "And Nari?"

The parasite nodded. "She chose clarity. She chose to embrace something greater than herself. And in doing so, she has never been more whole."

Liam exhaled sharply. "She would never give up her mind willingly."

"She did not give up anything. She made a choice. And now we offer you the same."

Silence stretched between them.

Liam looked down at his hands, covered in blood and ash. He had fought for so long, run for so long. He had watched people die, seen good men fall, lost everything for a world that didn't even know he existed.

And now—

They were offering him peace.

Liam's voice was hoarse. "Why are you doing this?"

The lead parasite's glowing eyes did not waver. "Because your world has already tipped the scales of balance. And you must understand why."

The shadows around them deepened, shifting like liquid. The walls of the facility melted away, the air rippling with energy.

A vision rushed into Liam's mind.

The Lost History of Nikri

Liam's consciousness lurched backward, flung into a world long gone.

The air around him shimmered, the underground bunker dissolving into nothingness. He found himself standing on a planet bathed in twilight, its sky a deep indigo. Towering structures of obsidian and metal rose high into the heavens, pulsating with an ethereal blue energy. Strange, beautiful creatures roamed the land, their movements synchronized, almost rhythmic—as if every living thing on this planet was connected by a single thread.

This was Nikri.

And then—

War.

It began with a tremor beneath their feet, a ripple of unease that spread like wildfire. The sky, once adorned with luminous celestial patterns, darkened as massive warships broke through the atmosphere. Metallic behemoths, their hulls gleaming with artificial light, descended like gods of destruction. The first explosion tore through the capital, sending debris raining down like meteor showers.

Panic erupted. The streets once filled with harmony became battlefields of despair. Families clung to each other as soldiers scrambled to defend their homeland. The Nikrians, though advanced in knowledge and technology, had never prepared for war. Their unity had been their strength, their greatest virtue—

—and their downfall.

The invaders were human.

Liam's stomach twisted as he watched the carnage unfold. The first wave was swift and merciless. Human soldiers, clad in exoskeletal armor, descended like a plague. Their weapons—unlike anything Nikri had ever known—spat searing plasma, reducing entire districts to cinders.

The Nikrians fought back the only way they knew how—with their connection to one another. Their telepathic bonds allowed them to move as one, reacting before bullets could reach them. They created shimmering barriers of energy, shielding their people from annihilation. For a moment, it seemed as though they could hold.

Then came the second wave.

Orbital bombardments rained down, obliterating entire regions. The great spires of knowledge, libraries containing centuries of wisdom, crumbled into dust. The very foundation of their civilization shattered. The golden rivers of Nikri, once flowing with pure energy, boiled and turned black.

Liam saw children running, their small hands reaching for parents who had already turned to ash. He saw warriors, desperate, pushing forward despite knowing they would never make it. He saw the Nikrian leader—the same being who stood before him now—standing atop a crumbling tower, his voice echoing through the broken city.

"We are one! We do not break! We fight for our home!"

The Nikrians surged forward, their unity forming a last, desperate defense. They hurled their energy against the invaders, disrupting their weapons, overriding their machines. Humans fell, their bodies collapsing as their own technology turned against them.

For a fleeting moment, hope flickered.

Then, the final blow fell.

A nuclear missile, launched from a hidden base on Earth, streaked across the sky.

Nikri's leader looked up, his glowing blue eyes reflecting the doom above. He raised his hands, commanding every last ounce of energy his people had left, forming a protective dome over the last surviving city. The missile struck—

And the shield held.

For a heartbeat.

Then it cracked. Shattered.

The firestorm consumed everything.

Nikri died in fire.

The vision shifted again, faster this time, showing Liam the aftermath.

The once-thriving cities were now nothing but rubble and radioactive dust. The few remaining Nikrians wandered the wastelands, their once luminous eyes dim with sorrow. But they did not give up. They evolved.

With their world gone, they had to survive. They learned to adapt, to merge with other life forms, to create balance where destruction threatened to reign.

"This is horrible," Liam whispered, his voice hoarse as the vision faded and reality snapped back into place.

The lead parasite's glowing eyes locked onto his. "That is why we sought to seek and create balance. We were never meant to control. We were meant to preserve what was left."

Liam stood there, his mind a storm of thoughts, the weight of history pressing down on him.

Balance. Control. What was the difference?

Chapter 11:
The Choice

The vision of Nikri's destruction faded, and Liam found himself back in the dim ruins of the underground facility. The weight of what he had seen pressed heavily on his chest, his breathing unsteady. His mind raced through the images—the fire, the death, the horror. And now, the beings before him—the last remnants of Nikri—stood in eerie silence, watching him with unreadable expressions.

Then, the silence broke.

Footsteps echoed through the cavernous room, and Liam's heart clenched as he turned.

Nari.

She emerged from the darkness, her presence almost ethereal. Her once warm brown eyes were now an otherworldly shade of blue, glowing faintly under the dim light. Her jet-black hair cascaded over her shoulders, but something about her was different—her movements were too fluid, too precise. She carried herself with an unnerving stillness, as if the air around her obeyed her presence.

"Liam," she said, her voice still familiar but layered with something else—an unnatural calm.

Liam's breath hitched. "Nari...?"

She stepped closer, tilting her head slightly. "You look exhausted. Have you been fighting again?"

A lump formed in Liam's throat. He wanted to rush forward, to take her hands in his, to shake her and demand answers, but he couldn't move. Instead, he forced his voice to remain steady. "Are you... still you?"

The parasites around them remained silent, watching intently. The leader, the one who had shown Liam the vision, finally spoke. "She is more than she was before. She is enlightened. Free."

Liam clenched his fists. "Free? She's—she's not even acting like herself! She's different!"

Nari smiled faintly. "I feel... clear. My mind doesn't fight itself anymore, Liam. I see things now, in ways I never could before. There's no fear, no hesitation, no pain. I am whole."

Liam took a step back, shaking his head. "No. That's not you. That's them talking."

Nari's expression didn't falter. "Is it? Or is this who I was meant to be?"

Liam turned sharply to the parasites, his voice filled with unfiltered anger. "Can she ever go back? Can she ever be normal again?"

The leader watched him carefully, then spoke with a quiet finality. "No. A parasite does not leave its host. And even if it did... she would not survive."

Liam's stomach twisted. He felt as if the ground beneath him had crumbled, leaving him stranded in a pit of helplessness. "So, she's just—gone? I'll never have her back?"

The female parasite stepped forward, her glowing eyes locking onto him. "She is not lost. She is still here, standing before you. Loving you, just as she always has. But she has evolved beyond what she once was."

Liam exhaled sharply, his hands trembling. "That's not fair..."

Nari took another step closer. "Liam, I know this is hard. I know it's terrifying. But what if this is the only way? What if fighting against it only brings more pain? I don't feel lost. I feel... right. And I don't want to do this without you."

Liam's eyes burned. "You still want me? Even like this?"

"Always," Nari whispered. "But I can't make the choice for you."

Liam turned to the parasites. "If I agree... what happens to me?"

The leader regarded him carefully. "You will be one of us. You will gain clarity, strength, and purpose. But you will not be the same."

Liam hesitated, his heart pounding.

His mind screamed at him to run, to fight back, to refuse—but another part of him, the part that had spent years in war, in isolation, in suffering, whispered something else.

What else do you have left?

Nari was gone, at least the way she had been. Darren was dead. The world he had fought to protect would never know his sacrifices. If he left, he would be alone.

Or... he could stay.

With her.

Liam took a deep breath, his hands curling into fists before he finally whispered, "What are your conditions?"

The leader's expression didn't change, but Liam swore he saw something close to satisfaction flicker in his glowing eyes. "One: We decide where you work. Two: We will remain in your mind, granting you strength. Three: It will change you, in ways you cannot predict. Four: There will be moments when we take control, when it is necessary. And five: We will come to you when we decide the time is right."

Liam's heart pounded. He turned to Nari, searching her face. "And you… you're okay with this?"

She nodded. "More than okay. I need you with me, Liam. We can be together. We can live… even if it's different from what we imagined."

Liam swallowed hard. The weight of his choice pressed down on him like an avalanche. But at the center of it all was her.

He had fought wars.

Lost friends.

Sacrificed everything.

But this... this was the one thing he couldn't bear to lose.

He turned back to the parasites, his jaw tightening.

"Fine. I accept."

The lead parasite gave a slow nod, as if it had always known the answer. "Then it is done."

The air around Liam shimmered as a presence stirred. The whispers grew louder, curling around his consciousness like vines. But he didn't fight it.

He was done fighting.

The parasites slowly began to fade into the darkness, their forms dissolving into the shadows. Nari stepped closer, taking his hand in hers. Her skin was cool to the touch, but it was still her. Still real.

"We have each other," she whispered. "That's all that matters."

Liam exhaled slowly, looking at her glowing blue eyes.

And for the first time in a long, long while—

He let go.

And embraced his fate.

Chapter 12:
The Rebirth

The night was eerily silent. The underground facility had long since gone dark, the remnants of destruction now nothing more than ruins. But within one of the remaining chambers, Liam lay in a cold bed, his body heavy with exhaustion.

For the first time in years, he allowed himself to sleep.

The dim glow of the moon barely reached him through a cracked window above. His breaths were deep, slow—unaware of the presence lurking in the shadows.

Something moved.

A shimmer in the air. A ripple, like liquid shifting against the silence. A shape, barely distinguishable, slithered forward.

The parasite.

It was unlike anything human eyes could comprehend. A sleek, dark form, its texture a mix of fluid and solid, an ever-changing state. It pulsed with an inner glow, a whisper of intelligence rippling through its essence. It had waited patiently. And now, it was time.

The creature ascended the bed frame, inching closer to Liam. Its movements were methodical, almost reverent, as if approaching something sacred.

Then, without hesitation, it slithered forward—

And entered.

A thin tendril curled into Liam's nose, winding its way through his sinuses, deeper, deeper. The sensation was neither painful nor suffocating, but it was there—a presence settling within him.

Liam stirred slightly, his fingers twitching against the sheets. His breathing hitched for the briefest second before steadying again.

The parasite sank into his mind.

A pulse shot through his body.

Something shifted.

His veins darkened for a brief moment beneath his skin, a faint glow spreading through them before vanishing. A deep, thrumming warmth coiled through his chest, threading into his very being. His heartbeat slowed—not weakening, but synchronizing.

Then, his eyes snapped open.

Gone was the warm brown that had once colored them. In its place, a deep, unnatural blue had taken over, the hue vibrant yet eerily cold. His pupils, once dark, now gleamed with a new intensity—not fully human, not fully alien. A mark of what he had become.

The process was complete.

Morning came.

Golden sunlight seeped through the cracks in the ceiling, casting soft patterns onto the bed where Liam lay. The room was quiet, peaceful—the first semblance of calm in what felt like an eternity.

A steady rhythm of breathing reached his ears. Not just his own.

His eyes fluttered open.

Nari.

She lay beside him, her form half-draped in the sheets, her dark hair splayed across the pillow. The glow in her blue eyes had dimmed, settling into something calm, knowing.

For a moment, neither of them spoke. They simply existed. Together.

Then, a smile curled at the edges of her lips. "You're awake."

Liam inhaled slowly. He felt... different. The exhaustion, the ache that had plagued him for so long, was gone. His senses were heightened—the air was sharper, the warmth of the sun more vivid. And yet, he felt completely at ease.

His hand instinctively reached up, touching his face. His skin felt the same, but beneath it... something had changed.

A deep sensation curled through him, something new. Something powerful.

He turned his gaze to Nari. "It's done, isn't it?"

She nodded slowly, watching him carefully. "Yes."

A silence stretched between them—one heavy with meaning. With realization.

Then, it began.

The shift.

Liam exhaled sharply, his body tensing as warmth spread through his limbs, a slow morphing taking place beneath his skin. His muscles tightened, reshaped—not growing, not mutating, but refining. His features sharpened ever so slightly, his complexion paling, his once newly-blue eyes now glowing with an even deeper intensity.

His hair darkened further, strands shifting as if touched by something unseen. His very presence felt stronger, heavier—otherworldly.

Then, he felt something else.

A shift beside him.

Nari gasped softly, her body reacting to the same unseen force. Her fingers gripped the sheets as a pulse of energy coursed through her, mirroring Liam's transformation. Her breath hitched, her head tilting back as a warmth spread beneath her skin, her very essence adapting, syncing, evolving.

Her once delicate features sharpened, the softness of humanity shifting into something more striking, more defined. Her already black hair deepened into an inky abyss, strands shimmering with a faint iridescence. Her eyes—once eerily blue—now burned with ethereal brilliance.

She let out a slow exhale, blinking rapidly as she adjusted to the changes. Liam watched, entranced, as her presence grew, expanded—matching his.

When it was over, they looked at each other.

And for the first time, they were truly the same.

The same power. The same clarity.

The same fate.

Nari smiled softly, her fingers tracing his jawline. "We're one now."

Liam let out a slow breath, his mind strangely at peace.

"We always were."

Chapter 13:
Reunion and New Purpose

Liam's eyes fluttered open, greeted by the soft, golden glow of the morning sun filtering through the sheer curtains. The warmth pressed against his skin, but it wasn't the sunlight that made his heart feel at ease—it was the steady rhythm of Nari's breathing beside him.

For a moment, everything was still. No battles, no parasites, no grand schemes of balance. Just them.

But as his consciousness sharpened, a faint hum vibrated through his mind—something new, something foreign yet familiar. The presence. It was there, woven into his very being, a silent observer yet undeniably a part of him now. He turned his head slowly and took in the sight of Nari lying beside him, her body curled slightly toward his, her dark hair spilling across the pillow. She looked peaceful, more so than she had in weeks.

And then he saw it—her eyes flickering open, revealing irises that glowed with the same haunting, otherworldly shimmer as his own.

A rush of understanding passed between them without a single word. They had changed.

Not just in body, but in purpose.

The weight of their decision settled into Liam's chest, but before he could dwell on it, a familiar, reverberating voice whispered in his mind.

"It is time."

The parasites had returned, or perhaps they had never truly left.

A ripple of static coursed through Liam's nerves, and suddenly, he knew where to go. As if an invisible hand guided him, a location, a destination, burned itself into his mind. He turned to Nari, and from the way she sat up and nodded, he knew she had received the same message.

No words were needed.

They dressed in silence, their movements synchronized yet effortless. Every breath, every step felt amplified, like their bodies had been recalibrated to a new frequency. Their connection was deeper than before—not just as partners but as something more, something neither entirely human nor entirely parasite.

As they stepped outside, the city stretched before them, unaware of the shift that had taken place. The world still spun in its endless cycle of chaos and order, but Liam and Nari had been reborn into something in-between. And they had a role to play.

A black car waited for them at the curb, sleek and silent. The moment they approached, the doors unlocked with a soft click. No driver. No instructions. Just trust in the path set before them.

They slid inside.

The moment the doors shut, the car began moving.

As they drove, Liam caught Nari's gaze in the reflection of the tinted window. A small, knowing smile touched her lips. Despite everything, despite the terror, the pain, the loss—they were together. And that was enough.

For now.

The vehicle pulled into an underground facility, hidden beneath the city's surface. As they stepped out, the walls around them pulsed faintly, veins of light running through them like living circuitry. The air was thick with something unspoken—knowledge, power, the presence of something vast and incomprehensible.

A towering set of steel doors loomed ahead. The moment Liam and Nari approached, a sharp chime echoed through the chamber.

"State your purpose."

The voice wasn't human. It wasn't even fully mechanical. It was something in between, just like them.

Liam glanced at Nari. A silent agreement passed between them. Then, as if instinctually knowing what to do, they reached out—not with their hands, but with their minds.

The world around them trembled.

The doors responded.

With a slow, deliberate groan, they slid open, revealing the heart of the organization that had orchestrated everything.

The Balance Keepers.

And Liam and Nari had just taken their first step into their new existence.

Chapter 14: Fractured Allegiances

Part 1: Shadows in the Glass

The city stretched before them like an endless sea of neon and darkness. Rain glazed the rooftops, softening the harsh glow of streetlights below. Liam crouched near the edge of the high-rise, his breath controlled, his pulse steady—just as it should be.

Beside him, Nari remained still, but something was different about her tonight. He could feel it.

Their target resided in the penthouse across from them, a man whose very existence threatened the fragile equilibrium the parasites sought to maintain. *Eliminate him. Restore balance.*

Liam's fingers curled around the grip of his silenced pistol, feeling the familiar weight in his hands. Every movement was calculated. Perfect. The parasite's will guided him, honed him into an instrument of their control. There was no hesitation—there never had been.

Until now.

He turned his gaze toward Nari. She hadn't moved. She was staring straight ahead, eyes locked on their objective, yet her finger hovered just above the trigger of her rifle. Not pressed against it. Just hovering.

A beat of silence.

Nari.

A whisper in his mind—his own voice, untouched by the parasite's interference. He hadn't meant to call out to her, but something inside him did it anyway.

Her fingers tensed. He saw the slightest tremor in her hand, so small that only someone who knew her better than himself would notice.

Then the parasite's voice slithered through their consciousness. *Execute. Now.*

The illusion of hesitation shattered.

Liam turned back, sighted the target, and pulled the trigger.

Part 2: The Illusion of Free Will

The muffled shot was absorbed into the sound of the rain, a whisper of death that left no room for error.

Inside the penthouse, their target staggered, a crimson bloom spreading across his chest before he collapsed soundlessly onto the floor.

A clean kill.

Liam exhaled slowly, lowering his weapon. Across from him, Nari remained frozen, still staring at the glass as if she were searching for something in her own reflection.

"We need to move," he murmured.

She blinked, as if just now returning to reality, and nodded. They withdrew from their positions, slipping into the shadows, the parasite's will guiding them effortlessly through the night.

And yet, something gnawed at him. A whisper beneath the surface.

A hesitation that should not exist.

As they descended through the building, exiting through an alleyway unnoticed, Liam felt his mind shifting back to equilibrium. The parasite's influence was an unyielding presence, smoothing over any questions before they could fully form.

And yet.

That flicker of defiance in Nari's hesitation...

Had she felt it too?

Part 3: Fractures in the System

The safehouse was sterile—void of warmth, void of anything resembling life. It was not meant to be lived in, only occupied when necessary.

Liam moved through the dimly lit space, stripping off his gear with practiced efficiency. Across from him, Nari stood near the sink, washing the blood from her gloves. The water ran red before spiraling down the drain.

He watched her, waiting.

She hadn't spoken since the mission.

"You hesitated." The words left his lips before he could stop them.

Nari's hand stilled under the water.

For a moment, she said nothing. Then, softly:

"You didn't?"

Liam frowned. "Of course not."

Her gaze lifted, locking onto his. There was something unsettling in the way she looked at him—not as a partner, not as an agent. Something deeper. Something dangerous.

"Then why are you asking?"

He opened his mouth, but no answer came.

The parasite stirred within him, sensing the disturbance. *Do not question. The mission was a success.*

A sharp exhale. The thought was buried. The doubt silenced.

And yet, as Nari turned back to the sink, fingers gripping the edge, he knew—

She was breaking.

And a part of him wasn't sure if he wanted to stop it.

Part 4: The Parasite's Mercy

Later that night, Liam lay awake, staring at the ceiling. The parasite's presence was a constant hum in his mind, a force of control that never wavered. And yet, for the first time, something else lingered alongside it.

A whisper of something foreign.

Doubt.

His training had conditioned him against it. His mind had been sculpted into an unshakable instrument of the parasite's will. And yet, here it was.

He turned his head slightly, glancing toward Nari. She was curled up on the opposite side of the room, her back to him, but he could tell—

She wasn't asleep.

"Nari," he said quietly.

She didn't move.

The silence stretched between them, an invisible force pressing down on both of them.

Then, barely above a whisper—so soft he almost didn't hear it—she spoke.

"Liam... do you ever wonder if this is real?"

His chest tightened. The parasite's grip flared, pushing against the thought, erasing the question before it could root itself in his mind.

Liam exhaled. His expression remained neutral.

"No," he lied.

A pause.

Then, softly, she whispered back:

"Liar."

And for the first time, Liam had no words to respond.

Part 5: The Weight of Acceptance

Morning came, and with it, a new mission. The parasite's control ensured that the questions of the night before were buried beneath fresh orders, fresh objectives.

But Liam and Nari knew. They had begun to see the cracks in the illusion, and though they obeyed, something within them had shifted.

As they prepared to leave the safehouse, Liam reached for Nari's hand, a small gesture that spoke volumes. She didn't pull away.

They were not free.

But they were together. And for now, that was enough.

Chapter 15:
The Prophecy Revealed—
A Cosmic Deception

In a startling revelation, Liam and Nari learn that they are part of an ancient prophecy—two destined saviors, bonded by love, chosen to restore balance to the world. As this truth unfolds, their very beings shift, reshaped by the cosmic forces that have long awaited their awakening. Their voices deepen with an unearthly resonance, their skin pales to an unnatural ivory, and their hair darkens into strands of liquid midnight. But the most striking transformation is their eyes—now radiant pools of cosmic blue, reflecting the power they unknowingly wield. They are breathtakingly beautiful, like celestial beings cast among mortals.

Yet, this divine metamorphosis comes at a steep cost: their free will.

The parasites, ever-watchful, tighten their grip, strengthening their control under the guise of enlightenment. With each passing moment, Liam and Nari's thoughts are guided, their emotions carefully curated. They find themselves enraptured in a state of euphoric bliss, their minds drowning in an artificial happiness that leaves no room for doubt, no space for rebellion. Their love, once their own, now feels amplified beyond human comprehension, a force so intense it erases all questions of choice.

They embrace their roles in the prophecy with unwavering devotion, genuinely believing they are fulfilling their ultimate purpose. The illusion is seamless. The joy they feel is real—undeniable, inescapable. They are not prisoners; they are chosen. They are not controlled; they are enlightened. They are not victims; they are saviors.

And yet, beneath this perfect illusion, a whisper lingers.

A whisper of something lost. A ghost of autonomy flickering at the edges of their consciousness, buried beneath layers of imposed purpose. But the parasites are masterful in their work. Each time such a thought dares to surface, it is smoothed away, replaced with a warm flood of certainty. Doubt is an anomaly, an impossibility. The parasites weave their influence like a masterpiece, allowing just enough of Liam and Nari's original selves to remain so that they never suspect the truth.

The world sees them as divine entities, beings of unfathomable beauty and wisdom. To their followers, they are saviors reborn, cosmic forces made flesh. The prophecy is unfolding exactly as foretold, and Liam and Nari stand at its center, radiant and resolute. They make their declarations with conviction, their voices carrying the weight of destiny. They move with grace, their every action precise and perfect. The world adores them. Worships them. And in their minds, they are at peace.

But peace built on chains is not truly peace.

The parasites have orchestrated this deception with meticulous brilliance. The depth of their control ensures that Liam and Nari will never resist, never even recognize that resistance is an option. To them, their love is stronger than ever, a beacon in the darkness. They believe their choices are their own, that their mission is righteous. And so, they move forward, fulfilling the prophecy without hesitation, unaware of the forces pulling their strings.

The deeper their belief, the stronger the parasites' hold. Each whispered doubt is drowned by a tide of manufactured certainty. Each moment of hesitation is seamlessly rewritten, the parasites molding their thoughts as an artist sculpts clay. Their love, raw and untethered, should have been their shield—but instead, it has been reforged into their shackles.

They do not question why they never feel sadness, why their joy is constant and unyielding. They do not recognize that true love comes with sorrow, that true devotion must battle doubt. Instead, they accept their roles without hesitation, convinced that their path is just, their actions righteous.

And yet, in the stillness of the night, when the stars bear silent witness, something lingers. A feeling. A fleeting thought. A second where Liam turns to Nari, and for the briefest moment, the world does not feel quite right. But before the thought can take shape, before realization can bloom, the parasites weave their magic once more. The unease vanishes, replaced with the overwhelming warmth of purpose. He smiles, and she smiles back, their hands entwining as they gaze upon the world they are destined to save.

The chapter closes with Liam and Nari standing together, their mesmerizing forms aglow under the stars. Their fingers intertwine, their connection unbreakable, their devotion absolute. They are celestial saviors, ethereal and divine. They are everything the world needs them to be.

And yet, they are nothing of themselves.

Blissfully unaware, they embark on their destined path, their hearts full of love, their minds no longer their own, forever ensnared in the grandest illusion of all.

Epilogue: Love's Eternal Symphony

Twenty years have passed.

Twenty years since Liam and Nari became something beyond human—something neither alive nor dead, neither free nor controlled. For two decades, they were guided by an invisible hand, never questioning, never hesitating. They lived under the illusion that they were righteous, that every choice was their own, that their love was untouched. And then, without warning, it all stopped.

The parasites let go.

There was no grand revelation. No reason given. One day, they simply awoke, and the weight that had always been there was gone. It should have felt like salvation. Instead, it felt like loss.

For the first time in twenty years, there was silence. And it was unbearable.

The world was still. Too still. Without the hum of purpose thrumming in their minds, without the gentle pull of an unseen force shaping their every decision, the emptiness stretched before them like a void. And in that silence, in that awful, crushing silence, they felt the truth sink in.

They had nothing.

Their past was a dream they could never return to. Their hands, once so sure, now trembled with the weight of everything they had done—every mission, every life taken, every choice they thought was righteous. Had they ever been heroes? Or were they only ever weapons, pointed at a target and fired?

They could have run from it. Started over. Left each other behind. Nothing bound them anymore—no prophecy, no force, no fate. They could have walked away and pretended none of it ever happened.

But they didn't.

Not because they had to. Not because they were meant to. But because even after everything—even after all the years of being controlled, of being used, of being molded into something unrecognizable—the only thing that still felt real was each other.

Their love had never been a choice. It had been forced upon them, shaped by something beyond their will. And yet, standing here now, stripped of everything, raw and exposed, they realized that for the first time in their lives—they could choose.

And they still chose each other.

But love was not enough to heal what had been broken.

Their freedom was not a gift. It was a graveyard of memories that would never fade, of years stolen and never returned. There would be no redemption. No justice. No fixing what had been done.

They would never be normal again.

And that was the hardest truth of all.

They had spent years believing in something greater than themselves. Believing that they were part of something bigger, something important. But there was no grand meaning. No ultimate reward. The world did not owe them peace.

There was only the road ahead, empty and uncertain.

And so, they did the only thing they could. They walked forward.

Not toward happiness. Not toward sorrow. Not toward any promise of salvation.

Just forward.

Because life is not a story of perfect endings. It is not a battle of good versus evil, nor a path to redemption.

It is only a collection of moments, some stolen, some given, and all of them irreversible.

And Liam and Nari, no longer heroes, no longer puppets, no longer anything but themselves, had learned the most painful truth of all.

There is no going back. There is only living with what remains.

And so, *hand in hand, they walk on—not into light, nor darkness, but into the quiet understanding that some wounds never heal, and that some love, no matter how broken, never fades.*

www.ingramcontent.com/pod-product-compliance
Lightning Source LLC
LaVergne TN
LVHW041608070526
838199LV00052B/3043